P9-DDC-995

Tommy Greenwald

Charlie Joe Jackson's Guide to EXTRA Credit

Illustrated by J.P. Coovert

Roaring Brook Press ✱ New York

For my parents

who showed me by doing

Published by Roaring Brook Press
Roaring Brook Press is a division of Holtzbrinck Publishing Holdings Limited Partnership
175 Fifth Avenue, New York, New York 10010
mackids.com

Library of Congress Cataloging-in-Publication Data

Greenwald, Tom.
Charlie Joe Jackson's guide to extra credit / Tommy Greenwald ; illustrated by J.P. Coovert.—1st ed.
p. cm.
Summary: Bright but unenthusiastic middle school student Charlie Joe Jackson signs up for the school play in an attempt to get straight As on his last quarter report card in order to avoid having to go to Camp Rituhbukkee over the summer.
ISBN 978-1-59643-692-3
[1. Middle schools—Fiction. 2. Schools—Fiction. 3. Theater—Fiction. 4. Interpersonal relations—Fiction. 5. Humorous stories.] I. Coovert, J. P., ill. II. Title.
PZ7.G8523Cg 2012
[Fic]—dc23

2011027820

Roaring Brook Press books are available for special promotions and premiums.
For details contact: Director of Special Markets, Holtzbrinck Publishers.

First edition 2012
Book design by Andrew Arnold
Printed in the United States of America by RR Donnelley & Sons Company, Harrisonburg, Virginia

10 9 8 7 6 5 4 3 2 1

INTRODUCTION

How I ended up trying out for the school play is actually a pretty funny story.

Because if you know anything about me at all, you know I'm not exactly a "school play" kind of guy.

In fact, the idea of doing the school play is right up there with reading a book on my not-to-do list.

Which makes the fact that I was standing there on the stage of our middle school auditorium, singing a song about paper towels, all the more ridiculous.

And just because the most perfect creature in the world was trying out too—Hannah Spivero, of course—didn't make it any better.

"5-6-7-8!" yelled Mr. Twipple, the drama teacher. Even though most of us had no idea what those numbers meant or why he was shouting them at us, we knew it meant we should start singing the song.

So we sang:

Wiping up messes!
Brushing off dresses!
There's nothing paper towels can't do . . .

I looked at my friend Timmy McGibney, who was there, too. He looked at me. We were both thinking the same exact thing.

How did this happen?

I'll tell you how.

Two words.

Extra credit.

Part One

I HATE REPORT CARDS

Charlie Joe's Tip #1

READ A LOT AND WORK HARD IN SCHOOL.

Reading and schoolwork are the backbone of every child's education.

It's extremely important to study hard and respect your teachers. The best way to make sure you get good grades is to do your work on time, and take great care and pride in everything you do. Try not to rely on extra credit if you don't have to, because it can turn out to be a very difficult process.

So, that's my first tip.

Or at least, it would be if we were living in fantasy land.

But we're living in real life, so ignore everything I just said.

Let's go back to the beginning: Report Card Day.

You probably already know that books and me don't get along.

And I'm not exactly what you'd call the most studious kid in the world.

In elementary school, that didn't really matter. I'd make my teachers laugh, and I'd participate in class, and I'd do just enough to get pretty good grades.

But everything changed in middle school. All of a sudden, the teachers expected me to actually read all the books and to pay close attention in class.

School turned out to be a lot more like school than it used to be.

Which is how Report Card Days became my least favorite days of the year.

"So what's the plan?" said my buddy, the ridiculously brilliant and unnecessarily hard-working Jake Katz. We were sitting at lunch. He asked me that every Report Card Day, as if I had some grand scheme to leave school in the middle of the day, go to my parents' computer, print out my report card (then delete the e-mail), find the nearest report-card-forgery expert and have him change all my C pluses to A minuses.

"I don't have a plan," I answered. Jake looked disappointed. I was pretty famous for my plans.

"My grades are definitely up this quarter," chimed in Timmy McGibney, my oldest and most annoying friend.

"That's super," I said, "but I don't want to talk about report cards right now."

I felt nervous, and I wasn't used to feeling nervous. I could usually get myself out of pretty much any bad situation, but going home to a lousy report card was kind of like going to a scary movie with your friends even though you hate scary movies. There was no way out.

I took a big swig of chocolate milk and immediately felt better. Chocolate milk is like that.

"Let's talk about something happy," I suggested, "like the fact that this is the last quarter of the year. Summer is right around the corner." Summer was my favorite time of year, by far. No school. No books. No report cards. There was absolutely nothing wrong with summer.

Then Hannah Spivero came up to our table and put her arm around Jake Katz, and I immediately felt worse again. Hannah Spivero is like that.

(Hannah, for those of you who have been living under a rock, happens to be the girl of my dreams. Only now, those dreams are nightmares, ever since she shocked the entire nation by deciding to like Jake Katz.)

Right behind Hannah was Eliza Collins and her adoring gang of followers, who I like to call the Elizettes. Eliza is the prettiest girl in school and has had a crush on me since third grade. The combination of those two things didn't make sense to anyone, especially me.

"Did I just hear someone mention summer?" Eliza asked. "What perfect timing! The girls and I have decided to form a Summer Planning Committee." Then she looked right at me. "It's coming up fast, and we need to make sure we have the best summer ever!"

Everyone cheered.

Eliza was used to people cheering in her presence, so she ignored it.

"The first meeting of the committee is this Saturday at my house, and you're all invited," she added.

Another cheer.

Hannah looked at Jake. "We have plans to go to the mall this Saturday."

I'll go to the mall with you, I thought.

"Maybe we can go to the mall on Sunday," Jake said. "The Summer Planning Committee sounds fun."

I couldn't believe my ears. Passing up alone time with Hannah Spivero went against everything I stood for as a person. "Okay, sure," Hannah said, but I could tell she was a little disappointed.

"What's wrong, Charlie Joe?" Eliza asked cheerfully. Since she liked me and I didn't like her back, seeing me unhappy always made her happy.

"Charlie Joe is feeling nervous about his report card,"

Timmy announced. He was another kid who enjoyed my misery.

"I am not."

Hannah put her hand on my shoulder, probably figuring she could help me forget my troubles and make me feel all warm inside from just the tiniest bit of physical contact. (She was right, but that's beside the point.)

"Oh, Charlie Joe, I'm not worried. You'll probably figure out a way to convince everyone that C's are the new A's. I'm sure your parents will be taking you to Disneyland by the time you get through with them."

Everyone laughed—it was a perfectly okay joke—but for some reason Timmy decided it was unbelievably hilarious, and instead of laughing he snorted apple juice through his nose and all over my fish sticks.

Great. Not only was I going to be nervous the rest of the day, I'd be starving, as well.

Timmy looked at the soggy fish sticks.

"Are you going to eat those?" he asked.

He'd eaten three of them before I could answer.

Charlie Joe's Tip #2

YOU CAN'T GO THROUGH LIFE THINKING YOU'LL GET EXTRA CREDIT JUST FOR DOING NORMAL STUFF.

There's extra credit . . . and then there's just regular credit. Getting regular credit for something just means you've avoided getting in trouble. If you want to actually get rewarded, you have to do more than what's expected. That's where the *extra* part of extra credit comes from.

Here are some things that I used to think would give me extra credit but didn't:

1. *Wearing matching socks*
2. *Turning in homework*
3. *Not swearing*
4. *Brushing my teeth*
5. *Eating salad*

As I went to put my tray away after lunch, I saw my unofficial best friend Katie Friedman talking to her friend Nareem Ramdal. They were in the gifted program together. The gifted program was supposedly to help challenge the really smart kids, but I think it might have been more for their parents, who could brag to their friends about it at dinner parties.

"I'm telling you, after Brian Jones died, the Rolling Stones lost some of their weird creativity that they never got back," Katie was saying to Nareem. He nodded, even though it was obvious he had no idea what Katie was talking about.

"Hey, sorry to interrupt," I interrupted.

Katie looked at me. "Charlie Joe, what's your favorite Rolling Stones song?"

"Um, I'm more of a Beatles guy. But I guess 'Satisfaction.'"

She shook her head. "What a cliché."

I pulled Katie over to the vending machine, which used to have candy and soda but now had vegetable snacks and tomato juice.

Katie was a little annoyed—she didn't like being interrupted when she was talking about classic rock. "What's up?"

"It's Report Card Day."

"Why do you insist on calling it Report Card Day? Nobody does that but you." Her phone beeped—incoming!—but she ignored it. "Are your grades going to be mediocre as usual?"

I wasn't exactly sure what mediocre meant, but I nodded. "Would I be talking to you if they weren't? I need to know what to say to my parents."

"Listen, Charlie Joe," Katie began, but her phone beeped again. It was clear she'd rather be texting her friends than talking to me about my bad study habits. "I can't really help you with this one. You're a really smart kid, but you hate to read and you hate to study. Your homework is always late and always lazy. And even in the easy classes, you find a way to get on the teachers' nerves all the time. So what do you expect? I'm not sure why four days out of the year you suddenly get all guilty and upset about it. It's who you are."

I thought about that for a second. "So what you're saying is I should tell my parents that they should just love me for who I am, lousy grades and all?"

Katie bought herself a bag of carrot sticks, which are like potato chips without the goodness.

"I think it's a good place to start," she said, chomping away like a very intelligent rabbit. "Where you finish is up to you."

I brought Pete Milano home with me after school because he was the one kid who could be counted on to make my report card look good. Pete had somehow figured out how to fail music, which takes talent.

"Dude, I will totally come with you," Pete said, when I invited him over. "The last place I want to be right now is at my house. My mom is going to be super ripping mad at me." Then he cracked up.

There wasn't all that much to admire about Pete Milano, but I had to admit, the way he didn't care about getting in trouble with his parents was pretty impressive.

When we got to my house, my two dogs, Moose and Coco, greeted me in the usual way—like I was a returning war hero. They don't care about C minuses. Which is one of the zillion things I love about them.

I noticed my mom's car in the driveway. She's a stay-at-home mom, so nothing unusual about that.

But then I noticed my dad's car in the driveway.

A lot unusual about that.

"Your dad's home," Pete announced.

"Yeah, I see that."

Dad being home wasn't part of the plan. The plan was to go inside, listen to my mom complain about my report card, and then tell her that I loved her so much, wanted to make her happy, and would totally do better next time. In other words, I would take advantage of her incredibly nice personality. Then later, she could help make Dad a little less mad.

Pete and I went inside, and there he was, sitting at the kitchen table.

"Dad!" I said, trying to sound completely thrilled to see him. "What are you doing here?"

"I had a meeting twenty minutes away, so I decided to work from home this afternoon."

Just my luck.

"Pete's here," I said, suddenly regretting my decision to bring home another kid who was famous for bad grades.

My mom came into the room, carrying a huge thing of laundry. (She once told me that she made a point to do housework when my dad was home, to remind him that he wasn't the only one who worked hard.)

"Hi boys!" she said as cheerfully as possible. Whenever things were tense in the house, Mom tried to be extra happy. "Can I get you a snack?"

"Pete, you should probably call your mom to come pick you up," my dad said.

"Oh, Jim, one snack," insisted my mom. Yay for moms.

"You don't have to make us anything, we'll just have cereal," I said, trying to score some brownie points. I looked at my dad to see if he was paying attention. "Then we're going to go play Ping-Pong."

Mistake.

"No Ping-Pong," my dad said. He got up from the table and stretched, like one of those lions you see on the nature channel, who's just waking up before going to kill a defenseless baby gazelle.

In case you were wondering, I was the baby gazelle.

Dad was holding a piece of paper in his hand, which he dropped in front of me. "Take a look."

No thanks, I'd rather not.

Charlie Joe's Tip #3

GRADES ARE OVERRATED.

It's nice to try to get extra credit to improve your grades, but it's not the end of the world if you can't pull it off. Because grades are totally overrated.

It's true. Studies have shown that there is no connection between a good middle school report card and success in later life.

Okay, we can move on now.

ENGLISH: B–
ART: C+
SOCIAL STUDIES: A
MATH: C+
SPANISH: B–
SCIENCE: C–
GYM: B–
DRAMA: C–

I tried to look on the bright side.

"Check out that Social Studies grade. And Spanish is up from last quarter."

My dad shook his head. "Charlie Joe, this is NO GOOD." (The capital letters mean he said it loud enough to make the dogs go into another room.)

"What I don't get is why you don't at least get A's in the easy classes," my mom added. "In my day, you could always count on things like music and art to get your grade point average up."

I tried to smile at my mom, who had been an average student just like me. "Yeah, well they're a lot harder now."

"I highly doubt that," said my dad, who had never been an average student in his life. "You don't read. You barely do your homework. And you don't respect the teachers. It's got to stop."

I glanced at Pete, who seemed confused. He was probably wondering why he'd avoided getting in trouble at his own house just to see me get in trouble in mine.

"Dad, I can explain," I began, but it turned out he wasn't all that interested in my explanation.

"I think it's time to have a meeting with your guidance counselor."

Wait, what?

But before I could actually *say* "Wait, what?" my mom jumped in.

"We just think it would be a good idea to meet with Ms. Ferrell."

Ms. Ferrell used to be my English teacher. Right after I was in her class, she gave up teaching and decided to become a guidance counselor. Draw your own conclusions.

"We just want to figure out a way to get those grades up a bit," my mom continued.

"More than a bit," my dad corrected.

My mom smiled at me. "You're so smart, Charlie Joe." This was the part where she felt guilty and needed to compliment me. "You have so much going for you. It shouldn't be that difficult for you to apply yourself just a bit more in school. Your grades would shoot up!"

Pete decided he needed to say something. "Hey, Mrs. Jackson, could I get that snack now?"

"Absolutely." As she started making him some mac-n-cheese, I remembered what Katie had said. It was worth a shot.

"You know what? I think my grades are fine. They might not be all A's, they might not even be all A's and B's, but they're not that bad. And I have news for you guys. There are plenty of people in the world who are rich and successful who didn't have amazing grades in middle school. It just takes people like us more time to mature, that's all."

I marched to the cabinet and got myself a bowl of cereal. "And if you love me for who I am, you'll just have to respect me, grades and all."

My parents didn't say anything, as Pete and I dug into our respective meals. After a minute or two it felt safe enough to change the subject. "I got some new paddles," I said to Pete. "Best two out of three?"

"You're on," Pete said, holding a noodle in his mouth for Moose to grab. They were best buds. I think Moose thought Pete was another dog.

After we finished our snacks, I made a big point of rinsing out our bowls and putting them in the dishwasher. My

mom went to put away the cereal. "Let me do that," I said, taking the box. Every little bit helps, right?

Wrong.

"We've already called Ms. Ferrell," my dad said. "The meeting's tomorrow at seven-thirty, before I go into the city."

I looked at my mom, who smiled sadly.

I shrugged. "Fine. Whatever."

Pete and I went to play Ping-Pong, but my heart wasn't in it. He beat me three straight.

I've always liked Ms. Ferrell, and I'm pretty sure she always liked me, but that didn't mean we always saw eye to eye on things.

Life, for example. We definitely didn't see eye to eye on life.

She saw life as a constant opportunity to learn, and to be amazed by literature, culture, society, and all sorts of things that make the world special.

Whereas I saw life as something to enjoy, without being distracted by annoying things like reading and writing and working.

But like I said, we really got along pretty well. I guess deep down I knew she had my best interests at heart.

Which made it pretty unusual that I was having bad thoughts about her.

To be specific, I spent the whole night imagining that she would have to cancel the meeting because she was suddenly stricken with a terrible case of gastrointestinal distress.

You know. Diarrhea.

The conference didn't start off all that bad. Ms. Ferrell told my parents how smart she thought I was, and how funny, and how they should be proud of my winning personality.

"He's a true original," was how she put it.

"Harrumph," harrumphed my dad, who didn't seem all that impressed.

"Well, we do think he's a funny, great kid," said my mom, looking on the bright side as usual. "But he needs to find a way to know when to be funny and when to be serious."

"There's plenty of time to be serious," I argued. "I have my whole adult life to be serious."

"Charlie Joe, enough!"

That was Dad. He had a pretty hot temper sometimes.

"Jim," my mom said to him quietly.

He took a deep breath. "All I'm saying is, enough is enough. Ever since you got into middle school your grades have been getting worse and worse. It's time to buckle down. It would be bad parenting if we just sat here while you threw your talents away."

Before I could decide if I wanted to argue or not, Ms. Ferrell reached into her desk and pulled out some sort of pamphlet.

"I do have an idea that you might want to consider."

I glanced nervously at the pamphlet. I was pretty sure it wasn't exactly an invitation to video game school.

My dad took a look at the front. "Camp Rituhbukkee," he said, smiling. "Am I pronouncing that correctly?"

Ms. Ferrell nodded. "Indeed."

I gagged. "Camp *Read-A-Bookie*? Are you serious?"

"It's a wonderful summer camp," Ms. Ferrell said. "With equal emphasis on sports and academics."

My dad thumbed through the brochure. "Looks interesting."

I was too horrified to form any actual words. This was my *summer* they were messing with! Nine weeks of heaven. The most important time of the year. So important that we had to form a Summer Planning Committee to plan it.

Ms. Ferrell looked at me. "Now, Charlie Joe, I know what you're going to say about the idea of going to a place like this. But I wouldn't suggest it if I didn't think you would enjoy it. Yes, it's got some classwork, but it's also a typical summer camp, with games and dances and all of that kind of stuff."

Poor, clueless Ms. Ferrell. She didn't understand that "games and dances" were just as much of a turn-off as "classwork."

But my dad was into it. "I really like the looks of this place, I have to say." He held out the brochure to me and grinned like an evil wizard. "Want to take a look?"

"No, thanks," I said, but he gave it to me anyway. It was filled with kids reading and writing and doing other school-type things. There was one kid in a canoe but he was wearing glasses and an oversized life jacket, and he looked like he would have been much happier with a dictionary than a paddle.

I tossed the brochure on the table and looked at my mom, begging her to speak up on my behalf, but I knew it was useless. The train to Camp Rituhbukkee was leaving the station, and my mom wasn't about to lie across the tracks to stop it.

But I was.

"What if I get straight A's this quarter?" I blurted out before realizing it.

No one said anything. I think they were all in shock.

"It's the last quarter of the year. How about if I get straight A's, you guys can't send me to Camp Life-is-suckee, okay?"

"Watch the language," said Ms. Ferrell.

"That sounds fair," said my mom, always ready to make a deal.

My dad snorted out a laugh. "Straight A's? You've never gotten straight A's in your life."

Good point, I had to admit.

"You say it all the time, if I only worked harder and concentrated on my schoolwork, I could get really good grades," I pointed out.

"That's a big *if*," Ms. Ferrell said. "The quarter started over a week ago, and you're already off to a shaky start."

"I know it's a big *if*," I answered, suddenly very determined to pull this off. "But if I can do it, I should be able to do whatever I want this summer, like sleep and watch TV and play with the dogs and hang out with friends like a normal kid, and not have to go to some stupid camp that's really more like school."

The three adults in the room all looked at each other.

"Straight A's?" Dad said.

"Straight A's with one B," I said, remember my hopelessness at Science. "I should be allowed one free B."

"A freebie!" my mom said, cracking herself up.

Ms. Ferrell's phone rang, but she ignored it. "Charlie Joe, if I'd known what it would take to get you to apply yourself in school, I would have shown your parents the brochure for this camp a long time ago."

My dad got up out of his chair and walked over to the

window, where he could see a bunch of kids getting off the school bus. Pete and Timmy were there, doing typical middle school things like jumping on each other, punching each other in the arm, and laughing like idiots.

Finally my dad turned around and looked at my mom, who nodded.

"It's a deal," he said.

Charlie Joe's Tip #4

YOU CAN GET EXTRA CREDIT AT HOME, TOO.

School is the number one place for extra credit, there's no doubt about it. But you can also get extra credit at home. And extra credit at home can go a long way. Doing one little nice thing for Mom and Dad can get you out of a lot of jams, trust me.

Here are some nice, easy ways to get extra credit at home:

1. *Take out the garbage (even when it's not your turn).*
2. *Feed the dogs. (Ditto.)*
3. *Make your bed. (Or at least spread out the top blanket so it kind of looks made.)*
4. *Bring the laundry basket down to the laundry room. (Don't actually DO the laundry though. That would be going too far.)*
5. *Set the table. (Plates are really all you need. Mom can do the rest.)*
6. *Turn off the video game without being told. (This is a tough one. If you can do it, you're a better man than I.)*

So go for the extra credit at home. It can get you out of almost anything.

Except for a meeting with your guidance counselor.

Okay, so I had a plan in place. Excellent!

Except for the fact that I had no idea how to pull it off.

Just so you can understand the difficulty of the road ahead, I should probably mention that the best report card I ever got was one sentence long: "*Charlie Joe is an intelligent, funny child with a bright future ahead of him, although he can be a bit mischievous at times.*"

That was in kindergarten.

As soon as I got home from the conference, I headed straight for my sister Megan's room.

Megan was in high school, and had been getting straight A's all her life. She loved reading. She loved doing homework.

Now that I think about it, it's kind of amazing we're related.

I figured she'd be a good person to talk to. I went into her room, and we lay down on her bed the way we have since she was seven and I was three. I explained the situation to her.

She bolted upright when I got to the good part. (Or should I say the bad part.)

"STRAIGHT A'S??!?!"

"It's not totally impossible."

"Charlie Joe, listen to me," she said. "I don't blame you. I wouldn't want to go to that camp, either, and I actually like school. But straight A's? You're crazy."

"I'm allowed one B," I mumbled, but that didn't seem to change her mind about the fact that I was out of mine.

"How are your grades so far this quarter?" Megan asked.

"Good."

"No, really."

"Fair."

"I thought so. Are you annoying your teachers?"

"Definitely not."

"No, really."

"Maybe a little."

She lay back down on the bed and whistled. Then she scrunched up her eyes, which meant she was thinking especially hard. "Well, here's the thing. You're definitely smart enough to get A's in the academic classes, especially if kids like Jake and Katie help you out. But how are you going to be able to get A's in Gym and Art? You're genetically incapable of behaving well enough to pull that off."

I didn't know what "genetically incapable" meant, but I was pretty sure it wasn't good.

"And doesn't your Drama teacher totally hate you?" Megan asked.

"I'm only taking Drama because I didn't want to take chorus," I said, which didn't really have anything to do with anything.

"Whatever," Megan sighed. She'd heard all my excuses before. "As far as I can tell, there's only one way for you to pull this off."

I knew it! I knew Megan would know what to do! She always had good ideas. She was a genius.

"Extra credit," she said.

"Extra credit?" I said.

"Extra credit."

Scratch that whole genius thing.

I was still getting used to the idea of working hard enough to get good grades. Now I was supposed to work *extra* hard?

"What exactly does that mean?" I asked Megan.

She picked up one of her stuffed animals and started throwing it up in the air, trying to avoid the ceiling fan. It was a game we'd played for years, and it was fun. It was especially fun when we'd miss, and the fan would catch one of her zebras or giraffes and send the poor thing flying against the wall with a big smack.

"What it means is, you've always been a loudmouth. And you're at the age now where if you talk too much in class, the teachers aren't going to find you cute, they're going to find you annoying. And if they already think you're annoying, it's going to be hard to suddenly make them be your best friends." She threw the turtle to me. "You're going to have to go out of your way to win them over. You need to ask them for extra credit."

I tossed up the turtle and the fan's propeller caught it perfectly, sending it crashing into an Albert Einstein poster.

"I don't get it. I'm supposed to ask Mr. Radonski if I can clean up the locker room or something? That's so gross. It's just not going to happen."

"It won't be cleaning the locker room. They have trained professionals for that. It's going to be some kind of special project, probably."

I tried to imagine asking my Gym teacher, Mr. Radonski, or my Drama teacher, Mr. Twipple, or my Art teacher, Ms. Massey, what I could do to get an A in their classes.

The thought of it almost made me throw up in my mouth a little.

"I don't know. I just don't think I can do it."

"It's not that big a deal. Tons of people do it. It shows that you care and that you're trying and that you're dedicated to making yourself better in school."

I picked up Megan's poor, bruised little turtle and put it on top of her sixteen pillows.

"But I'm not any of those things."

12

The next day, I decided I needed to have a meeting with my advisory committee.

And in middle school, when you need to have a meeting, there are two options: lunch and recess.

But unfortunately, lunch that day was turned into one of those assemblies where some weird dance troupe comes into the cafeteria and starts jumping around and imitating trees. Afterward, the principal, Mrs. Sleep, gave a speech telling us all how important the arts are and why they matter so much.

I agree, the arts are awesome, and they totally matter a lot, but not when I need to have a meeting. And besides, if the people in charge of the school system want kids to love the arts, they should hire like a rock band or a comedian or Emma Stone or something.

You could interrupt lunch for Emma Stone. I'd be okay with that.

In any case, I had an urgent matter to attend to, and since lunch was kidnapped by strange dancers, that left recess.

I assembled my group of advisors underneath one of the basketball hoops. There was Jake and Hannah; Katie; Timmy; and Pete, who was a perfect person to listen to, because whatever he suggested, you did the opposite.

Katie's super smart friend Nareem was there, too. I think Katie brought him because she figured I could use all the brainpower I could get.

"I've been going to Camp Rituhbukkee for five years," was the first thing Nareem said. "I totally love it."

"You're not helping," Katie told him.

"This is a waste of time," Timmy announced. He was completely useless in terms of giving me advice. I'd known him for so long, he was almost like a brother to me. Which just meant he enjoyed my problems far too much to ever want them to go away. "There's no way you can get straight A's," he went on. "We'll sure miss you on the Summer Planning Committee." He laughed and high-fived Pete, completely unnecessarily.

Nareem took off his glasses and started cleaning them.

"So what you're saying is that because your parents are insisting upon your attendance at camp, which you consider really just a school in disguise, you have decided to formulate a plan by which you improve your grades through a combination of diligent studiousness and assistance from friends."

Nareem was from India, which meant he spoke much better English than the rest of us.

"I guess so," I said.

Hannah looked concerned. Even though she'd broken my heart by becoming Jake's girlfriend, it meant I got to spend much more time with her, and she'd become a pretty good friend. Which was kind of like being allergic to ice cream and then moving above an ice cream store.

"No one should have to go to summer reading camp, Charlie Joe, especially you," she said. "Jake, Katie, Nareem, and I can definitely help you get your grades up."

Pete and Timmy looked at each other. I think they didn't know whether to be mad that Hannah didn't include them, or relieved that they didn't have to help me.

"Absolutely," Jake said. He credited me for setting him up with Hannah, so he was always willing to help me out. "There haven't really been any tests so far this quarter, so as long as you do your work and study with us, you'll be fine. Dude, you're totally smart enough to get this figured out."

(By the way, Jake never used the words *dude* and *totally* before going out with Hannah. Getting to date the most perfect girl in the world sure can change a guy.)

Katie still looked skeptical. "You have to work harder than you ever have in your life. Can you do that?"

"I think so," I said. I didn't have a choice. There was no way I was going to that camp.

"And Science can be your B," Hannah pointed out, stating the obvious. The day I got an A in Science would be the day my dog Moose decided he didn't like steak.

"This is boring," Pete said, picking up a basketball. Then he and Timmy started playing a game, which involved slamming the ball against the backboard so hard it ricocheted to the other side of the court. Whoever gets it the farthest wins.

I watched them for a minute, then turned back to my friends. "I also need to get A's in Drama, Art, and Gym."

"Oh, jeez," said Jake.

"Uh-oh," said Katie.

"Yikes," said Hannah.

"That's a horse of a different color," said Nareem.

We looked at him.

"It means *yikes*," he added.

I started pacing around. "I know, it sounds crazy. My sister thinks the only way I can do it is if I asked my teachers for extra credit."

From the basketball court, Timmy and Pete guffawed. "Extra credit!" snickered Timmy. "That's extra hilarious!" bellowed Pete.

Nareem whistled. "I must say, Charlie Joe, that you do

not strike me as the type who would be able to ingratiate yourself with your teachers in any sort of meaningful way," he said.

"I would agree if I knew what *ingratiate* meant," Jake said. If Jake doesn't know a word, you know it's a pretty incredible word.

"It means to suck up to someone," Nareem said, which made Pete and Timmy laugh all over again.

"Oh," said Katie. She looked at me. "Yeah, you're definitely not the type to go ingratiating yourself, that's for sure."

"I know," I said. "That's my point. I need you guys to help me figure out some kind of extra credit thing to do."

"Maybe you could volunteer to put away the art supplies," Hannah suggested.

"Or maybe you could tell Mr. Twipple you'd be willing to stack the chairs in the auditorium every day after school," Jake offered.

"Or maybe you could sweep the gym floor," Nareem added.

Everybody started shouting suggestions at once. Meanwhile, one of Pete's throws missed the backboard entirely and hit poor Tessa Burns in the right ear. When she screamed bloody murder, Mr. Culpepper marched over and took the ball away, so Pete and Timmy wandered back over to us.

After listening for a minute, Pete pretended to punch

me in the face, and then actually punched me on the arm. "You guys got it all wrong. You don't get to pick the extra credit stuff. The teachers do. That's how it works. You go up to them and ask them how you can get extra credit in their class. Then hopefully they'll tell you what to do to get your grade up. Any dummy knows that."

We all stopped talking. Pete was absolutely right. Perhaps for the first time in his life.

We all looked at him in shock.

"What?" Pete said.

"Good idea, Pete," said Jake, since the rest of us were speechless. "Charlie Joe, you should start by talking to Mr. Radonski after Gym class."

Everyone nodded except Timmy, who had to throw in one last snarky comment.

"Good luck with that," he said.

Lame, but snarky.

Charlie Joe's Tip #5

IF YOU'RE DOING EXTRA CREDIT FOR A TEACHER, YOU HAVE TO LIKE THEM. (OR AT LEAST PRETEND TO LIKE THEM.)

The whole point of doing extra credit is to make a teacher like you, so that hopefully they'll give you a good grade. But you're kind of blowing it if you don't like that teacher, because they'll be able to tell, and then they won't like you back. So, even if you think a teacher is kind of annoying, you have to make it seem like they're the greatest person in the world.

Here are a bunch of ways you can pretend to like a teacher:

1. *Laugh at their jokes (especially when they're not funny).*
2. *Nod when they're talking.*
3. *Ask questions in class.*
4. *Say hi when you come into the classroom, and bye when you leave.*
5. *Say "that's a very good point!" a lot.*
6. *Ask them if you can have them again next year (knowing full well that you can't).*

7. *Skip the apple—what they really want is a chocolate chip cookie from the cafeteria.*
8. *Notice the picture of their family on their desk, and say how good-looking they are.*
9. *Don't fall asleep in class.*
10. *If you do fall asleep, don't snore.*

Of course, after the extra credit project is done, the two of you can go back to staying out of each other's way.

"I want to see intensity out there! I want to see hustle! I want to see you leave it all on the floor! Everybody ready? And . . . PLAY!"

Mr. Radonski, the Gym teacher, blew his whistle loud enough for people in New Guinea to hear it, and we started the game.

Football? Basketball? Wrestling? Ultimate fighting?

Nope. Badminton.

See, the thing about Mr. Radonski is, he's kind of crazy. Even though badminton feels more like a nap than a sport, he treated it the way he treats everything: like a combination of a World Series and a World War.

Plus, it was Opposite-Hand Thursday. Meaning, every Thursday, no matter what sport we were playing, Mr. Radonski made us play with our opposite hand. He was totally hyper about teaching kids how to become ambidextrous. Which probably seemed like a good idea at the time, but trust me, it wasn't. The only good thing about it was that it made the jocks and the non-jocks equally horrible.

Katie and I were playing against Timmy and Eliza Collins. Because she was so pretty, Eliza was the only one who could get away with anything less than maximum effort. So annoying.

I served the birdie with my left hand. I barely made contact, and it went about three inches. Eliza watched the birdie flutter to the ground and giggled.

"You're supposed to hit it back," I said.

She stuck out one of her long, perfect fingers. "It was way over there."

She threw the birdie at me. I threw it back, and it hit her softly in the right toe.

"OW!" she screamed. As if anyone would believe she was actually in pain.

Mr. Radonski did. He stormed over to our court, his chest sticking out in that funny way that makes him impossible not to imitate.

"JACKSON! What do you think you're doing?!"

"There's no way that hurt," Katie offered. Thank God for people like Katie Friedman.

"When I want your opinion, Friedman, I'll ask for it," Mr. Radonski barked. I actually kind of liked that he called girls by their last names, too. He was kind of an equal-opportunity insane person. "So what happened here?"

"He threw the birdie at me. With his RIGHT hand," said Eliza.

Why is it that girls who have a crush on you like to show their love by doing whatever they can to get you in trouble?

He grabbed my racquet. "Collins, throw me the birdie." She threw it to him in that uncoordinated, underhanded way that girls use to tell people that they're way too girly and adorable to bother with stupid things like sports.

"Nice throw," Mr. Radonski said, completely missing the point. He turned to me. "Now look here, Jackson. Ambidexterity isn't a laughing matter. Being able to do things with your weak hand is important in sports, and in life." He then whacked a lefty serve right by Nareem Ramdal's right ear.

He handed the racket back to me. "Try it."

I threw up the birdie and proceeded to swing and miss three times. Mr. Radonski squinted at me.

"You're doing that on purpose."

"I'm not, I swear."

"Try it again."

I gave one more mighty left-handed swing, but the racket slipped out of my hand and bonked Mr. Radonski on the side of the head.

"ARGH!"

Nobody moved, and everyone was dead silent, for like thirty seconds. Then someone had the nerve to giggle. We all turned and stared at the giggler: it was the new girl, the one who always wore a braid in her hair. She'd just started school like three days before and obviously didn't know yet that Mr. Radonski was a complete psycho. She turned bright red.

He glared at her. "What are you laughing at?"

"I forget," she said, twirling her braid and sneaking a smile at me. I smiled back at her. Even though she was new, she looked familiar.

Mr. Radonski interrupted the moment.

He stuck his chest into my face. "SPORTS are LIFE! And LIFE has two kinds of people. WINNERS and LOSERS!" Then he tossed the racquet back to me in disgust. "If you want to be a loser, Jackson, that's up to you."

He walked away, sticking his chest out extra far.

I turned to look for the new giggling girl, but she was gone.

Meanwhile, Katie came over to me and bonked me over the head with her racquet.

"Good luck with that whole extra-credit thing," she said.

Charlie Joe's Tip #6

IF A TEACHER IS GIVING YOU EXTRA CREDIT, DO NOT INJURE THEM IN ANY WAY.

Do as I say, not as I do.

Mr. Radonski's office looked like a kid's room. There were piles of clothes everywhere, bats and balls on all the furniture, and sports posters on every wall.

On his desk was a calendar with inspirational phrases on it, like "Play Outside, Grow Inside" and "Exercise Your Body, and the Mind Will Follow."

I knocked, a little too loudly. Mr. Radonski nearly jumped out of his chair. He seemed surprised to see me. I would have been surprised to see me, too, considering I'd just thrown a badminton racquet at his head.

"Jackson! What the—?" He caught himself before he finished the sentence.

"Is this a bad time?"

"Well, it's not great. I was just checking the schedule for this year's Board of Ed softball team. It's a big year; we gotta take back the title from the Parks and Recreation guys. We're gonna kick 'em in the teeth this year! Mark my words."

I tried to sound excited. "Consider them marked."

Mr. Radonski looked me up and down, trying to figure out if I was being a wise guy.

I looked back at him as sincerely as I possibly could. It turned into a staring contest.

I lost.

"What can I do you for?" Mr. Radonski finally said, satisfied at his victory.

I cleared my throat. "Well, Mr. Radonski, first of all, I wanted to apologize for hitting you with the badminton racquet."

He waved his hand in the air. "What else is new?"

I laughed, just in case he was trying to be funny. Then I just stood there, until he noticed I hadn't left.

"Is there something else?"

"Well," I stammered, "what I want to say is, um, I mean I was wondering, I think it would be awesome if I could, well—"

"Just say it, little man."

"Do you think there's any way I could get extra credit in this class?"

Mr. Radonski let out this huge laugh that scared the heck out of me. He jumped out of his chair, ran out to the hallway and screamed, "Hey everyone! Charlie Joe Jackson wants extra credit in Gym!"

He came back into his office. "Oh, that is rich, my friend, that is rich. You spend the whole year pushing all my buttons, having your fun, getting on my last nerve, and now all of a sudden you want to be my little helper?"

"Yeah, sorry about all that stuff. I was being stupid."

Mr. Radonski shook his big bowling ball head back and forth. "I don't know, Jackson, I just don't know. You kids today, you're full of mystery, aren'tcha?"

"I guess." There didn't seem to be too much mystery about it, though. I needed an A in Gym, and I was going to do whatever it took to get it.

He fake punched me. "So, what's the deal? Your parents coming down on you hard about your report card, is that it?"

"Pretty much. They're really mad right now. If I don't get my grades up I might have to go to a camp for kids who like to read."

He groaned. The one thing I had in common with Mr. Radonski was that he would have hated that camp as much as me. "Ouch," he said, pointing to a chair. "Have a seat."

After I moved a basketball, a football helmet, a baseball bat, and three lacrosse balls out of the way, I sat down.

He picked up one of the lacrosse balls and started bouncing it against the wall. "So you want some extra credit from old Mr. R., do you?"

"I sure do."

He tossed a piece of paper at me. "SGC."

I looked at it. "SGC?" I asked, even though I knew exactly what it was.

"Student Government Council. It meets every Wednesday and Friday after school for an hour. I'm the staff advisor with Mrs. Chelton."

I looked at him, still not exactly sure what he had in mind. I think my brain was just trying to protect me.

Mr. Radonski leaned in close enough for me to smell the onions he'd had for lunch. "I want you to join the SGC. We could use a kid like you, who's always full of ideas. They're usually crazy ideas, but even so." He shifted in his chair, which gave out a sad squeak. "Besides, we got an open slot. One kid just quit, because he couldn't handle the pressure."

Was that supposed to encourage me? Because it didn't.

Mr. Radonski give me a smack that was supposed to be playful, but was actually kind of painful. "You join the SGC, we'll see what we can do about your grade."

I sat there, not sure what to do. A drop of sweat trickled down my cheek. This wasn't what I had in mind. I was thinking something more along the lines of putting away the soccer balls after class. But this was a much bigger deal. Student government? The kids who make the rules that other kids are supposed to follow?

It was the opposite of everything I stood for as a person.

Not to mention, you might as well just stamp the word *Dork* across my forehead.

I considered my options. A summer in hell? Or a one-way ticket to dorkdom?

I looked at Mr. Radonski. He looked at me. Another staring contest.

"I love politics," I said.

The newest member of the Student Government Council—that would be me—then trudged to the art room, where Mrs. Massey was rinsing out some paint brushes in the sink. She didn't hear me come in. Mrs. Massey was a very nice person, a very sweet person, and a very kind person. She was also a very deaf person.

See the thing about Mrs. Massey was, she was about ninety-two years old. I think she'd been teaching Art at middle school since before middle school was invented.

And not only was she totally old, she was totally old-fashioned. She still believed that A meant exceptional, B meant good, C meant average, D meant below average, and F meant failure.

So when she gave me a C plus back in the second quarter, and I complained to her about it, she said, "Why? It means I think you're above average in Art, Charlie Joe. Only slightly above average, it's true, but above average just the same."

To tell you the truth, I don't think I'm above average in Art. I'm probably quite a bit below average, and I may also have participated in a paint fight or two in class, I can't quite recall. In any case, I think she was just being nice.

It's a little sad when your teacher gives you a C plus just because she's being nice.

I waited while Mrs. Massey cleaned the brushes. When saw me, she gave me a huge smile. "Charles Joseph!" she exclaimed. "How wonderful to see you here in the studio!" She called the Art room "the studio," for some reason. I think it reminded her of the old days. She liked to talk about the old days a lot, back when she was an artist in some part of New York City called SoHo.

She frowned. "Have I forgotten an appointment? It wouldn't be the first time."

"No, Mrs. Massey. I just wanted to come see you and talk to you for a minute."

"Wonderful! I love company."

She walked behind her desk and stood in front of a huge poster of a sculpture of a naked lady who was missing her arms. On the first day of school, we all broke into a huge fit of giggles when we saw it, until she shushed us by saying it was one of the most important pieces of art ever created. That shut us up for about twenty-eight seconds. Then we started giggling again.

Mrs. Massey took one pair of glasses off and put another pair of glasses on. (I think the older you get, the more pairs of glasses you need. My grandmother has a pair of glasses for every room of her house.)

"To what do I owe the pleasure?" Mrs. Massey said, sitting down.

I sat down, too. "Well, first of all, Mrs. Massey, I want you to know that you're definitely one of my favorite teachers."

"That's very sweet."

"But I know I'm not the best artist in the world, and I really, really want to do well in this class." I shifted in my seat. "So, I'm wondering, is there anything I can do to help get my grade up?"

She reached into her desk and took out a folder. "Let's see here, Charlie Joe. You have been averaging about a C or C plus in my class for the year. You're not a terrible Art student by any means, but you do tend to get distracted quite a bit, and your effort so far this quarter has been somewhat lackluster. So obviously, the first thing you need to do is work harder."

"Oh, I will," I assured her. "But I want to do more than that. I really want to make sure I can get an A, which is why I was thinking I could do extra credit."

"Ah . . . the grand tradition of extra credit." Mrs. Massey smiled as she put away the folder. "That's very dedicated of you, dear."

It wasn't about being dedicated, it was about being at the beach—but she didn't have to know that.

"There may be one way you can help me," Mrs. Massey continued. "I have been looking for a model, and you might be just the man for the job."

A model? The only models I knew were beautiful girls in bathing suits, and guys who looked like movie stars.

"I'm pretty sure I'm not good-looking enough to be a model," I said.

Mrs. Massey laughed and coughed at the same time, in that classic older-person way. "Oh, come now, Charlie Joe. You're a fine-looking boy. And I'm not talking about that kind of model."

Huh?

Mrs. Massey stood up. "Come with me."

We walked over to her bookshelf, which was packed with all sorts of huge books on painting and sculpture and photography and stuff like that. She pulled out a book and started flipping the pages until she found what she was looking for.

"Here," she said, pointing at the page.

It was a painting of a boy wearing some sort of weird outfit, with a red vest, a strange hat, green shorts, and a tight checkered jacket that looked really, really uncomfortable.

"Who is this kid?" I asked.

"This 'kid,' as you call him, is Byron Chillingsworth, a very famous boy foxhunter in nineteenth-century England. He will also be the subject of my next painting."

I still wasn't sure what any of this had to do with me.

"I would like you to pose as young Mr. Chillingsworth."

Oh.

That's a new one.

"Um, what does that mean exactly?"

Mrs. Massey patted me reassuringly on the arm. "It's the easiest job in the world. All you have to do is sit for several hours a few days next week, while I paint you."

That didn't sound so bad.

"You can't move a muscle," she added.

That sounded kind of bad.

"And you have to wear hunting clothes," she double-added.

That sounded very, very bad.

"But I don't have any hunting clothes," I said, hoping for some reason that that would get me out of it.

"Oh, not to worry," Mrs. Massey said. "I will have a complete wardrobe for you."

I looked around the room, suddenly wondering what I was doing there and how I could escape. But there was no escape. Like it or not, I was going to become Byron Chillingsworth, boy foxhunter.

"Do I at least get to hold a gun?" I asked hopefully.

Mrs. Massey shook her head. "Oh no, my dear. Young Byron used a crossbow. But obviously, it's against school regulations to allow the students to handle any kind of weapons." She clapped her hands together happily. "But if you're lucky, I'll let you hold the hunting horn."

Oh, goodie.

Charlie Joe's Tip #7

EXTRA CREDIT IS GOOD PRACTICE FOR BEING AN ADULT.

One time my dad came home from work and announced that he got a big promotion. We all congratulated him, and he said, "Don't congratulate me. Congratulate Bruce Springsteen." It turned out that the boss of my dad's law firm is a huge Bruce Springsteen fan. My dad found out, called his buddy who works at the arena, and got his boss these incredible seats for Bruce's concert. The next day, he got the promotion.

Middle school or middle-aged, extra credit never goes out of style.

Shall we recap?

My report card was lousy, my parents threatened to send me to a reading camp for the summer, I joined the Student Government Council, and I agreed to sit incredibly still for three hours a day pretending to be a boy fox-hunter.

And we're just getting started.

Charlie Joe's Tip #8

PICK THE EASIEST SUBJECTS FOR EXTRA CREDIT. AND MAKE SURE IT DOESN'T INVOLVE READING.

This seems obvious, but a lot of people don't get it. It's simple: don't go for extra credit in the hard classes. That would just mean more hard stuff to do. Think about it: Do you actually want to do MORE Science or Math than you have to? So, if you can, stick to extra credit in the easy classes, like Art and Gym.

BUT . . . if the time comes when you have to get extra credit in, say, English, try to pick the easiest project possible.

The teachers usually decide what the extra credit assignment is going to be. But if you're lucky—which, in case you didn't know, I'm not—they give you a choice. And it's very important to make the right choice.

For example, your English teacher might tell you that there are two ways you can get extra credit. One is to read an extra book by the assigned author. And the other is to write a poem for the school magazine.

Is there really any question which one you should pick?

Write the poem. You can get it done in like four minutes.

Here, you can use this:

Roses are red
Violets are blue
I don't like homework
Can I go now?

See? It doesn't even have to rhyme.

Leave the reading for the kids who don't need extra credit in the first place.

Mr. Twipple, who taught Drama, was one of those teachers you either loved or hated, depending on the kind of person you were.

If you were totally into singing and acting and hugging and being all dramatic, then you thought Mr. Twipple was a genius.

If you were more like a normal person, then you thought Mr. Twipple was kind of a strange guy who always wore turtlenecks and hummed to himself a lot.

I've never considered myself a singer, actor, hugger, or hummer, but there I was, in Mr. Twipple's Drama class. It wasn't like I had a choice. Well I did, technically; I could have taken Chorus. But Chorus was with the wildly over-enthusiastic Mrs. Pitlow, who liked to have extra rehearsals twice a week *before* school. That was so never going to happen. So I wound up in Drama.

From the beginning, Mr. Twipple and I weren't exactly best buddies.

The first problem was when I got in a fight with this annoying kid, Evan Franco. Evan thought he was an amazing actor, and did everything he could to suck up to Mr. Twipple. Eventually I had to say something.

"Mr. Twipple, what's the deal with Evan Franco? I bet he would shine your shoes if you let him."

"That's not your concern, Charlie Joe," said Mr. Twipple.

"Yeah, mind your own business," said Evan, who unfortunately happened to be standing behind me. "Go read a book."

Read a book? Those were fighting words. So I had to fight back.

"You're a terrible actor," I said to Evan.

"Well, you couldn't act sad if your dogs died," he answered.

I pushed him against the blackboard. I had to; I had no choice.

Mr. Twipple gave me detention for three days. And Evan and I have been enemies ever since.

Then there was the time when the assignment was to pretend to be someone we thought was the complete opposite of ourselves.

I picked Mr. Twipple.

Probably a bad move, especially since he didn't particularly appreciate my imitation of his squeaky voice (which was pretty accurate, if you ask me).

Anyway, he gave me a C minus last quarter, and when I asked him about it, he called it "a gift."

But now the time had come to go to him and beg for mercy. Or, at least, extra credit.

He was in his office grading papers and singing along

with something on YouTube that had a lot of people dressed up like giant stuffed animals.

"Cats," he said, when he felt me over his shoulder.

"Cats are okay, but I prefer dogs."

He sighed. "*Cats*! One of the greatest musicals of all time."

"Cool," I said, although what I meant was, uncool.

Mr. Twipple put down his pen and looked at me. "What's up?"

Deep breath time. "Well, Mr. Twipple, I know I haven't exactly been the greatest Drama student so far, but I'm really starting to enjoy it and I think I might want to take it next year, too." The first half of the sentence was true, at least.

"Glad to hear it, Mr. Jackson," said Mr. Twipple, and he returned to his papers and his fake cats.

"The thing is, though," I continued, "in the meantime, I'm hoping it's not too late to get my grade up this quarter. To an A, if possible." I stopped to make sure he didn't fall off his chair. He didn't, so I continued. "And so I was wondering if there was any way to get extra credit in this class to help me do that."

Mr. Twipple looked like he was considering the most important question ever asked by anyone in the universe.

"I don't think so," he said.

Well, at least he was being honest.

"Really?" I asked. "I'll do anything."

"Charlie Joe, watch and learn." He pushed a few buttons on his computer, and up popped a video of some old guy saying a bunch of words I couldn't understand, even though they were definitely English.

I could swear Mr. Twipple had tears in his eyes. "This is the late John Gielgud," he said, "one of the greatest Shakespearean actors ever to grace the stage."

We watched some more.

"And, when I listen to Sir John, I remember why I got into this business."

It didn't seem like a great idea to point out that one of the world's greatest actors ever and a middle school Drama teacher weren't necessarily in the same business.

I tried to look impressed. "Yeah, he seems incredible."

Mr. Twipple abruptly turned it off. "He didn't become John Gielgud by asking his teachers for little favors. He became John Gielgud by working his butt off every day of the year, every year of his life. He never stopped working. He never stopped training. He worked incredibly hard, right up until the day he died."

"Wow," I said. As in wow, that sounds like the opposite of fun.

I watched and waited to see if Mr. Twipple would change his mind, but he went back to grading his papers. I got up to leave and was at the door when I heard him say, "There is one thing."

I turned around.

Mr. Twipple smiled. "The school play."

That's it? Easy-peasy! I nodded enthusiastically. "Great, thanks! I will totally come and see the school play. Absolutely. Looking forward to it."

He let out a combination of a laugh and a snort.

"I'm not talking about *coming* to the school play. I'm talking about *being in* the school play."

I waited a minute to see if he was kidding. He wasn't.

"Well, um," I stammered. "I've never really been in a play before. I can't really act, as you've seen for yourself."

"Ah, but that's where you're wrong," Mr. Twipple said. "You have talent. You can act. But you've been too busy acting *out* to know it."

I tried another strategy. "I think I'd be too nervous. I'd forget all my lines and stuff."

"You, nervous? The great Charlie Joe Jackson? I don't think I've ever seen you nervous in my life."

That was as close to a compliment as I was ever going to get from him, and I didn't want to ruin the moment, so I said, "Well, I guess I could maybe think about it."

Meaning, absolutely, positively, definitely, one hundred percent *not.* I'd rather go to reading camp for a full year than be in the school play.

"Good," Mr. Twipple said. "The auditions are in two weeks."

I had to figure out a way to be living in another state by then.

Charlie Joe's Tip #9

DO YOUR HOMEWORK ON TIME.

I learned this the hard way, but it's true. If you do your homework, you won't have to do a lot of extra credit.

It doesn't even have to be perfect. It's just has to be on time.

How hard can that be?

Pretty hard, as it turns out.

I've always been late turning in my homework. I've had excuse after excuse—I think my best ever might have been when I said it burned in the solar eclipse—but none of it mattered. The teachers subtracted points, my grades went down, and the next thing I knew, I was fighting for my grades, my summer, and my overall well-being.

So do your homework in front of the TV. Do your homework while texting and playing video games at the same time. Do it while you're sleeping, for all I care. Just do it on time.

It's so worth it.

Saturday. The day of the Summer Planning Committee meeting.

Yippee.

Considering that in two days I was scheduled to report for duty as Byron Chillingsworth, boy foxhunter, I wasn't exactly in the mood to go talk about what an awesome summer it was going to be. But then Eliza told me that she would be serving pizza and cupcakes.

Pizza and cupcakes happen to be two of my favorite food groups.

When I got there, there was absolutely no summer planning going on. Timmy was trying to show Jake how to play lacrosse, which wasn't going well at all. Pete wasn't there, because apparently he got grounded—I guess failing music was the last straw. And Hannah, Eliza, and the Elizettes were sitting on the porch staring at a computer, cracking up at a YouTube video of some girl who's trying to walk her giant dog, but ends up getting dragged across a Little League field and crashing into the pitcher. I guess it was one of those videos that gets funnier every time you watch it, right up until the zillionth time.

"Charlie Joe!" Hannah said, giving me a hug, which

immediately made the trip worthwhile. "We weren't sure you were going to come, with all the summer drama and stuff."

"Yeah well, there's no way I'm going to that camp," I said, looking around. "Um, where's the pizza?"

Eliza flipped her hair, which was her signature move. "Should be here any minute." She waved at someone behind me, and I turned around to see Katie walking up the driveway. She was with Nareem and the new, kind-of-familiar girl who had giggled when my badminton racket hit Mr. Radonski in the head.

"Hey," said Katie. "You guys know Nareem." He nodded and blinked a lot, like he couldn't believe he was actually at Eliza Collins's house.

Katie put her hand on the new girl's shoulder. "And this is Zoe Alvarez, who just moved back to Eastport after living in Boston for six years."

"Welcome back," said Jake.

"Nice to meet you," said Eliza.

"The Red Sox stink," said Timmy.

Suddenly I realized why I recognized Zoe.

"Hey," I said, going up to her. "I remember you. You were in my kindergarten class."

She tilted her head. "I was?"

"Yup. You were the girl who cried when Hammy died." Hammy was the class hamster.

"You remember that?"

"Yup," I said. "You yelled and screamed and had a tantrum to make sure we buried him properly."

Zoe blushed. "Oh, Jeez. Yeah, I've always had a bit of a bad temper, I need to work on that."

"Well anyway, I remember being really happy that you were crying, because that meant that I wasn't the only one."

Her eyes went wide. "That was you? Wow! I totally remember you, too! I remember thinking it was cool that a boy would cry over a hamster."

My turn to blush. "Yeah, well. I'm kind of an animal person."

"Me, too! I love all animals. But especially dogs. I have two."

"Me, too!" I said. "Moose and Coco."

"That's awesome." Then she laughed. "I remember you crying one other time, too."

"Uh-oh. You do?"

"Yup," she said." When Mrs. Calico tried to get you to read out loud."

"Oh. Yeah, that's entirely possible," I said, and she laughed again.

Then we ran out of things to say, so we just looked at each other for a minute.

"Well, really nice to meet you, again," she said.

"You, too." For some reason, though, I didn't want the conversation to end. I desperately tried to think of something else to say.

I came up with, "Hey, I never thanked you for taking some of the heat off me with Mr. Radonski the other day."

"Are you kidding? That was totally hilarious," she said. "I had no idea that Gym teacher was such a crazypants."

"That was nothing. One time he screamed at me for chewing gum in class. He yelled so loud his gum fell out of his mouth and into Kelly Crocker's hair."

We cracked up. Then we just looked at each other again. Zoe smiled. I smiled back.

"Oh, I remember that chewing gum thing!" said Hannah, who appeared out of nowhere. She took Zoe by the arm. "It's so great to see you again! Here, come with me, I want to show you the funniest video I've ever seen in my life."

As they walked toward the other side of the porch, Zoe looked back at me and smiled again.

Then Hannah looked back and gave me a funny look.

Katie was watching the whole thing. "Holy smokes, is Hannah channeling Eliza?"

I looked at her. "Huh?"

"If I didn't know better, I'd say Hannah was acting a little jealous there for a second."

"That's ridiculous," I said, unable to consider the possibility. Then I tried to consider it. "You think?"

Katie made that face she makes when she's about to say something really smart. "All I know is that girls like to have guys all to themselves, even guys they don't even like. Hannah has come to rely on you being in love with her. The idea of you actually liking someone else would not make her happy at all."

I thought about that for a minute. Hannah jealous? Over me?

I liked how that sounded.

Sadly, the Summer Planning Committee meeting went downhill from there.

I don't really want to go into details, because it would just remind me how miserable I was listening to everyone talk about how spectacular the summer was going to be, while I sat there wondering if I'd even be around to enjoy it.

The only good thing was that every time I tried to talk to Zoe, Hannah would interrupt. Maybe Katie was right. Maybe Hannah actually *was* jealous.

I kind of liked the idea that she wanted me all to herself, even if she didn't want the actual me.

Hey, it was better than nothing.

Charlie Joe's Tip #10

EXTRA ISN'T ALWAYS GOOD.

Extra credit is good. So is extra whipped cream. And so is extra sleep.

But that doesn't mean extra is always a positive thing. Sometimes it's definitely a negative. Like when you go to buy a new video game system, and then you want a game to go with it, and the guy behind the counter goes, "that'll be extra." As in, extra money out of your pocket. That's bad.

Here are a few other extras that are definitely bad:

1. *Extra homework*
2. *Extra chores*
3. *Extra-terrestrial (if the alien is trying to kill you)*
4. *Extra! Extra! Read all about it! (No thanks, but be sure to let me know when they make a movie out of it.)*

Part Two

THE CRAZIEST WEEK OF MY LIFE

There's this phrase, "Time flies when you're having fun." It means that life goes by too fast when things are nice and easy.

You know what the opposite of that phrase is?

The week I was about to have.

MONDAY

At breakfast, I told my mom that I needed to be picked up from school at four-thirty.

"How come?" my sister Megan asked. Even though she was the one who had given me the idea to go for extra credit, I hadn't filled her in on recent events.

"I'm going for extra credit," I said.

Mom clapped her hands together. "That's wonderful!"

Megan looked at me. She was always able to sniff out a good story. "What exactly will you be doing?"

"I'm not sure."

"Well, I'm sure it will be something fun and worthwhile," said my mom, who always looked on the bright side of things.

But Megan wasn't about to give up. "Which class?"

"Art." I brought my bowl to the sink, sending a signal that the conversation was over. The signal went unnoticed.

"I used to love Art class," said Mom dreamily. My mom loved everything about her childhood. If you believe everything she says, she was the happiest kid in the history of humankind. On the other hand, if you believe everything my dad says, his childhood was such a struggle that it's amazing he lived long enough to have his own children.

Megan followed me out of the room, bringing her cereal with her. "So what does Mrs. Massey have you doing?"

I somehow managed to get my ridiculously heavy backpack on my back. (Who's the genius who decided that all textbooks had to be four hundred pages?) "Posing for a painting."

Megan's eyes went wide. "No way!"

"Way."

"What are you posing as?"

"Stop asking so many questions!" I snapped. "I don't know! Just leave me alone!"

Megan looked hurt. "Jeez, sorry. I was just curious, that's all."

I looked at her and suddenly realized I was being a jerk. It wasn't her fault. She was a great older sister who was just trying to help, after all.

"A boy foxhunter," I said.

She laughed with a snort, and a single Cheerio shot out of her mouth and flew across the room.

"That's the most ridiculous thing I ever heard," she said.

Sometimes you need to stick with your first instinct and be a jerk.

I reported to Mrs. Massey's studio right after school. A part of me was hoping that maybe she was too old to remember our agreement, but there she was, setting up all her painting stuff. Her brushes were neatly laid out. So were the clothes I was supposed to wear, which were red, green, and tiny. I tried to imagine where Mrs. Massey had found them.

I decided that somewhere there was a frightened Christmas Elf running around naked.

I stood in the doorway, dreaming about turning around and running home as fast as I could. But right when I got to the part where I was sitting in front of the TV with four bags of fruit snacks spread out in front of me, Mrs. Massey looked up and spotted me.

"Charlie Joe! Right on time!"

"Hi, Mrs. Massey. It's me, Byron Chillingsworth."

She laughed and waved me over to the table where the clothes were. I looked at them, unable to pick them up.

"You want me to put those on?"

"That's why they're there, silly." She slapped the top of my head, which is something only teachers over sixty years old are allowed to do.

I headed out to change, but as I was leaving the studio I nearly crashed into a girl who was coming in.

Zoe Alvarez.

Not good.

"Hi!" she said, with a big smile. "Nice to see you again!"

"You, too," I said. "Sorry about almost running you over."

"No, it was totally my fault." Then Zoe bent down, picked something up and held it out to me, smiling. "I think these are yours?"

It was the tiny pair of shorty-shorts that I was supposed to wear. I hadn't realized I dropped them. At that moment, I wanted to bury them. And myself.

"Thanks," I said. "It's a costume."

"I kind of figured," she said.

She smiled again as I walked away. She liked to smile a lot, I noticed.

Changing in the bathroom was an adventure. I could barely get the green shorts on, they were so tight. There was also a white shirt, a red vest, a checkered jacket that was way too small, and a hat that looked like Peter Pan's.

I looked in the mirror. I laughed, until I remembered

it was me. Then I kind of cried a little inside.

When I went back to Mrs. Massey's room, Zoe was still there. She smiled again, of course. Mrs. Massey clapped her hands together in delight.

"Ah, Charlie Joe, you look fabulous! Perhaps you know my granddaughter, Zoe? She's also a painter, and will be joining me in this exercise."

My life flashed before my eyes.

"I know that wasn't part of the deal," Mrs. Massey said. It was like she was reading my mind, which probably wasn't hard, considering my mind was screaming **THAT WASN'T PART OF THE DEAL!!!** "But she really wants to learn the finer points of portraiture," Mrs. Massey continued, "and this will be a wonderful opportunity for her. I'll be forever grateful to you if you allow her this chance."

Right then, I wanted to teach Mrs. Massey the finer points of cursing, but somewhere deep inside of me I realized that this was a way to clinch my A grade for sure. If I let Zoe paint me while I was in this ridiculous outfit, Mrs. Massey would owe me big time.

"Fine," I said.

"Wonderful! Let's get to work."

Mrs. Massey told me to stand up straight and look out the window. Then she handed me my hunting horn.

Zoe looked at the horn and raised her eyebrows.

"If your dogs could only see you now," she said.

Charlie Joe's Tip #11

DON'T FALL FOR SOMEONE WHILE DOING EXTRA CREDIT.

This is a very important tip. Don't get a crush on a girl (or guy) while doing extra credit. First of all, it's like eating ice cream while doing homework. You can't really enjoy a good thing if you're doing a bad thing at the same time. They just don't belong together. And secondly, it can make you take your eyes off the prize. When you're doing extra credit, you don't need any distractions. Get the job done, and move on.

So basically, what I'm saying is, don't mix business with pleasure.

At least if you can help it.

You get to know people really well when you're posing for a painting in a red vest and tiny green shorts.

About an hour later, I knew that Zoe had moved away because of her dad's job, and moved back because her parents got divorced; that she used to be a horseback rider until she injured her back in a bad fall; that her dogs were named Pablo and Vincent, after two famous painters; that she loved scary movies but only watched them in the daytime; that her favorite food was fried chicken and her favorite drink was white grape juice (whatever that was); that the one thing she wanted to change about herself was her bad temper; and that she took up painting after her mom gave her a book by someone named Claude Monet and she thought his paintings were the most beautiful things she had ever seen.

Meanwhile, she learned that I was a lot less interesting than she was.

Mrs. Massey didn't say much. She liked to concentrate on her painting. But she did laugh at all my jokes, which was nice.

"Ten more minutes and we'll be done for the day," Mrs. Massey finally announced.

I sighed. "Oh darn, over so soon? I was kind of hoping to sleep in these clothes tonight."

Zoe laughed, and then reached down to pick up a tube of red paint. I noticed that the tube had a rip in it, but before I could say "Careful," she squeezed the tube, and red paint spilled all over Mrs. Massey's desk.

"Oh, my gosh," Zoe said. "Oh no."

"Shhh," I whispered, pointing at Mrs. Massey, who hadn't noticed a thing. Sometimes having an old teacher came in handy.

Zoe ran to the sink in the corner of the studio and got a bunch of paper towels to clean up the mess. She handed the garbage to me and without Mrs. Massey noticing I was able to shoot it right into the garbage can. Zoe giggled. "Nice shot," she whispered.

And for just a split second, I forgot I had a massive crush on Hannah Spivero.

The split second ended with a BANG! Meaning, an actual bang. Somebody was slamming something against the window.

It was Pete Milano, and the thing he was slamming against the window was himself.

"Take a hike!" I shouted.

"You look freakin' awesome!" Pete shouted back, laughing like a crazy person. "Can I have that vest when you're done with it? I'm going to be Superdork for Halloween this year!" He pounded the window with his hand. Then he turned and waved, and in about five seconds ten other kids from the soccer team were at the window, staring, pointing, and laughing.

Zoe looked at Pete carefully. "What's that kid's name again? He's in our Gym class, right?"

"Pete Milano. Don't bother with him, though, he's a real pain in the—"

"Mr. Milano, I'm going to have to ask you to let us be," Mrs. Massey said, trying to be heard through the glass. "Art demands concentration."

"Let us be, let us be," Pete sang, butchering The Beatles. "We're painting silly pictures, so let us be-ee-e—e." Everyone howled as Pete took a bow, and then they all ran away.

The three of us stood there in the silence for a minute, before Mrs. Massey announced, "Back to work."

Zoe was still staring at Pete. "I think I recognize him. Did he go to kindergarten with us?"

"Yup, and he hasn't changed a bit," I said, before picking up my horn and getting ready to not move for a few more minutes.

"You're a born foxhunter," said Mrs. Massey, as she moved her eyes back and forth from me to her canvas. "Dare I say you were born in the wrong century?"

"Did they have report cards in the nineteenth century?" I asked.

"I'm not even sure they had proper school, except for the very rich," Mrs. Massey answered.

I managed to look at her without moving my head. "Then I was definitely born in the wrong century."

When my mom picked me up, she asked me how it went.

"Fine," I said. "Actually, not horrible. Mrs. Massey's granddaughter is painting me, too, and she's really nice."

"Sounds like a fringe benefit to me," she said.

"I don't know what that means."

"It means that artists often fall for their subjects. And vice versa."

"That's hilarious."

"Thank you, dear."

I turned the radio louder. "Oh, and Pete Milano and half the soccer team stood at the window and made fun of me. That was awesome."

She turned the radio softer. "Jeez. Well, I'm very proud of you, Charlie Joe."

"Thanks, Mom," I said. Then, while her pride was still fresh, I added, "Can we go get some ice cream?"

"Absolutely."

Moose and Coco were in the backseat. They looked proud of me, too. Not for posing for a painting, but for getting Mom to buy me ice cream.

Mom got a vanilla cone. The dogs and I split an extra-large sundae three ways.

TUESDAY

Mr. Radonski still had a big red lump on his head when he showed up for Gym class.

"Try not to do any damage today, Jackson," he said.

Everybody laughed louder than necessary.

We were still doing badminton, and I was doing my best to be the perfect student.

But it turns out being the perfect student is just really, really hard.

Today's game was me and Katie against Nareem and Eliza. I served to Eliza. She hit it back to Katie. Katie hit it back to Nareem. Nareem hit a lob back to me, which was a perfect setup for a kill. I smashed it down the line past Eliza, who squealed in fake fear. We won the game.

I jogged up to Mr. Radonski, who was sitting on one of his high stools, watching another game. "Did you see that? I crushed that shot, it nearly took Eliza's head off!"

He looked down at me. "So you smashed the birdie at a girl?"

"Um, well, no. Actually I smashed the birdie PAST a girl."

"It was really scary," Eliza said. I couldn't believe it. Was she actually trying to make Mr. Radonski mad at me again? And more amazingly, was he actually going to fall for it again?

Mr. Radonski rubbed his bruised head. "So you think it's fun to frighten a helpless girl?"

Yup, he was going to fall for it.

"Girls aren't helpless," offered Katie.

Mr. Radonski glared at her. Then he glared at me. "You never stop, do you?"

I tried to resist the temptation to argue. I really did. But I couldn't quite pull it off.

"I don't get it, Mr. Radonski. I was just playing hard, the way you teach us every day. Like you always say, there are two kinds of people, winners and losers. And today, I was lucky enough to be a winner." I turned to Eliza. "Sorry if I *scared* you." Then I rolled my eyes, Katie Friedman–style.

My little speech had made the entire class stop what they were doing and stare at me. Nareem looked petrified. But Katie nodded, which made me feel relieved. If my speech was good enough for Katie, it was good enough for me.

Unfortunately, it wasn't good enough for Mr. Radonski. "Jackson," he said, squinting his eyes in pain, "why is it every time I think one thing, you think the opposite?"

"What do you mean?"

"I mean, yes, there are winners and losers. But sometimes,

part of being a winner is knowing how to lose. You try your hardest, but you play fair."

Suddenly Zoe stepped forward. "That's ridiculous, Mr. Radonski. All Charlie Joe did was hit the ball over the net. Eliza was just pretending to be scared. The freakin' birdie wasn't anywhere near her."

The class gasped. The new girl had talked back to Mr. Radonski! No one said a word. Not even Mr. Radonski.

Finally Eliza stepped forward. "It's true," she said. "It wasn't very near me at all. It was actually a really good shot."

Mr. Radonski looked around the class. I think he was in too much shock to do anything, so he just kept shaking his head.

I looked at Zoe. She mouthed the word "crazypants."

I laughed, unfortunately.

Mr. Radonski snapped his head toward me. "WHAT IS SO FUNNY NOW?" he thundered.

"Nothing."

He stared at me for what felt like a week. "Class dismissed."

And he walked out of the gym.

Nareem let out a huge breath and sat down on the gym floor. "I must say, that was one of the most traumatic encounters I have ever experienced," he said.

I went over to Zoe.

"How do you do that?"

"Do what?"

"Be incredibly, awesomely brave like that."

"I don't know," she said. "I can't help it. And my parents wouldn't call it brave. They'd call it stupid."

Katie came over. "I used to think you had nerve," she said to me, "but Zoe is one tough mama."

Timmy smacked Zoe on the back, which was his highest compliment.

The only one who didn't seem all that impressed by Zoe's courage was Hannah.

"You're lucky you didn't get detention," she said.

The rest of the school day was pretty uneventful, although I did pass Ms. Ferrell in the hallway between lunch and Spanish.

"Hi, Charlie Joe!" she said, brightly.

"Hey," I said, unbrightly.

She stopped me. "Charlie Joe, I know you're mad at me about the camp thing," she said. "I was only doing what your parents asked me to do. They're looking for ways to motivate you, and they finally found one. Mr. Suyama told me your Math grade is already up, Ms. Berk told me your Spanish homework has been excellent, and I heard you got a 96 on your English quiz."

I shrugged. "I still don't think you should have done that. Thanks to you, my summer might be ruined."

She sighed. "I'm just trying to help you reach your full potential."

"I hate potential," I said.

After school, Mrs. Massey and Zoe were all ready to go. I headed to the bathroom with my Byron outfit, ready to change into a different century.

Pete Milano was in there, eating lunch.

I asked the only logical question. "Why are you eating lunch in the bathroom?"

He took a bite of his sandwich and shrugged. "I forgot it was there until I went back to my locker at the end of the day, and I figured I'd eat it real quick before practice," he said. Or at least, that's what I think he said. It was hard to tell, because he was talking with his mouth full.

As I went into a stall, he pointed at my costume.

"Are you getting into those hilarious clothes again?" Pete asked.

I shut the door without answering, since I thought the answer was pretty obvious. When I came out, Pete was gone, but he'd left a note on the mirror:

ENGLISH DWEEB.

It was written in peanut butter.

31

Back in the studio, I asked Mrs. Massey and Zoe if they would show me their paintings so far. Mrs. Massey said no—she was superstitious about showing anyone a painting before it was done—but Zoe was happy to show me hers.

In case you were wondering, looking at yourself pretending to be a boy foxhunter in a painting is definitely one of the weirder experiences in life.

But the painting was good. Really good.

"That's amazing," I said.

Zoe smiled. "Thanks, Byron."

"She's a talented girl," Mrs. Massey said. "She's not going to be a teacher, like I am. She's going to be an actual painter."

"Stop it, Grandma."

I felt kind of cool that I was posing for someone that might be a professional painter someday. Maybe Zoe would become famous, and her painting of me would be in a big art museum someday. People would pay a lot of money to come see me!

I'd look like an English dweeb, but still.

***

After about twenty minutes, Mrs. Massey announced that she wanted to paint outside, to take advantage of the late afternoon light.

I immediately felt a panicky rumble in my chest. "Outside where?"

She pointed towards the fields, where Pete and his band of marauders were running around. "On the hill there. It's just catching the sun. Glorious!"

"Um, I don't think so," I said.

"Those kids are really annoying," Zoe said, coming to my rescue. "And with the sun coming through the window, it's really pretty right here."

But Mrs. Massey wasn't buying it. "Nonsense. Fox hunters hunted outside! We're not going to let a few silly boys stop us from making art."

"Mrs. Massey, I really don't want to," I begged.

She squinted at me. "Do you want extra credit in this class, or don't you? Be brave. You're a foxhunter!"

So out we went.

As soon as the soccer kids saw me, they started making comments.

"Can I borrow your underpants? I mean, shorts?"

"Nice vest! Where's the dork convention?"

"Looking foxy, fox boy!"

Mrs. Massey and Mr. Betts, the soccer coach, got them to be quiet, but that only lasted until I picked up the hunting horn and started posing.

First Pete came over and stood right behind me, striking the same pose, using one of the orange cones from the soccer field as his hunting horn. Then a couple of the other kids followed him.

"Leave us alone," Zoe said. Her voice sounded a little strange, like she just swallowed something gross.

Pete held the cone up to his mouth like a megaphone. "I shall not!" he bellowed, right into my ear.

"Ignore him," said Mrs. Massey, who marched away to get Mr. Betts.

I was glad she said that. Because the truth was, I didn't have the nerve to yell at Pete right then. I wanted to, but I was frozen. I hate to admit it, but I was a little scared, actually.

Have you ever tried to stand up for yourself while wearing a red vest and green short shorts? It's not easy.

Which meant, of course, that I ended up looking like a wimp in front of Zoe.

After another minute, Pete got bored and decided to annoy Zoe. He stood behind her while she painted and made stupid faces.

"Dude, that is one ugly fox hunter," he said.

Zoe turned around to face Pete. "Get out of here before I paint your face," she said. And she meant it. I was beginning to see a little bit of that temper she was talking about.

Pete wasn't sure what to do. I'm pretty sure a girl had never talked to him like that before.

"Fine," he said. But as he ran back to his practice he knocked the hunting horn out of my hand.

"Whoops, sorry about that!" Pete hollered, not at all sorry.

"How can you stand that kid?" said Zoe.

"Good question," I answered.

We got back to work. But no more than thirty seconds later, Zoe threw down her brush, yelled "I knew it!" and sprinted over to the soccer field.

I ran after her, but she was really fast.

And really mad.

Zoe ran right up to Pete, who was busy balancing a soccer ball on his nose like a seal. All the other kids scattered. Pete, whose eyes were on the ball, never saw her coming.

She looked like she was going to run him over, but she stopped approximately two inches from his face. "I knew I knew you!" she yelled.

Pete nearly jumped out of his skin. As he backpedaled away from Zoe, he tripped over the ball and fell flat on his back.

Zoe stood over him. "Not so brave now, are you, tough guy?"

Pete looked up at Zoe, a little freaked out. "W-What do you think you're doing?" he stammered.

"I knew I knew you from before, but I couldn't figure out how. But when you knocked the horn out of Charlie Joe's hand and said, 'Whoops, sorry about that,' it all came back to me."

Pete was still on the ground. I think he thought he was safer there. "What came back to you?"

The rest of the soccer team came over to see what was going on. Mrs. Massey and the coach were on their way over from the other side of the field. I figured Zoe had about thirty more seconds to make her point.

"We went to kindergarten together," she told Pete. "I was really shy and didn't really have any friends. But one day you came up to me in the playground and dared me to jump from one sandbox to another. I was so happy that someone was talking to me that I said sure. But just as I was about to do it you pushed me, and I fell into the huge mud puddle that was between the sandboxes. Right in front of everybody! All the kids laughed and laughed and laughed. I cried my eyes out. It was the worst day of my life."

I kind of remembered the incident Zoe was talking about. That was her? Uh-oh. Pete's in big trouble.

Zoe bent down so she was eye to eye with Pete. "And when I looked up at you to help me up, or be nice, or at least say sorry, guess what you said?"

"This is stupid," Pete said. He finally got the courage to stand up, but he looked a little sick to his stomach.

Then he looked at me. An easier target.

"You're gonna let a girl fight your fights for you?" he said. "Huh? You in that dumb little outfit? Just like in gym class, you're too scared to stand up for yourself, you have to let her do your dirty work for you? Huh, Mr. Fox-hunter?"

Pete started walking toward me. I froze. He was mad. He was bigger than me.

And the worst part was, he was right.

But just in time, Zoe came between us.

"I asked you a question," she said to Pete. "When I asked you to help me up, guess what you said?"

It was pretty clear Pete didn't feel like guessing, but Zoe didn't seem to mind. Instead, she picked up the soccer ball and kicked it right into his . . . into his . . .

Well, his you-know-where.

"ARRRGGH!" Pete screamed as he doubled over, in the kind of pain only a ball in the you-know-where can provide. The other kids were laughing hysterically because, well, it was the kind of comedy only a ball in the you-know-where can provide.

Mr. Betts ran up. "What do you think you're doing??!?" he yelled at Zoe.

She looked at Pete, then at the coach, then finally back at Pete.

"Whoops, sorry about that," she said.

After all the excitement was over, we decided to go back and paint inside after all. I expected Mrs. Massey to be angry, but all she did was chuckle a little bit and say, "Once a hothead, always a hothead."

"He had it coming," Zoe insisted.

"That he did," Mrs. Massey agreed.

As I sat there in my foxhunting costume, I closed my eyes, imagining I could go back in time. Not that far back. Only about thirty minutes, so if the same exact thing happened I could be as brave as the actual Bryon Chillingsworth, and not as pathetic as Charlie Joe Jackson pretending to be Bryon Chillingsworth.

I opened my eyes and saw Zoe right in front of me. It was still the present. And I was still a scaredy-cat.

I tried to smile. "I'm really sorry. I totally would have handled the Pete thing, but I didn't want to make Mrs. Massey mad."

"That's smart," Zoe said, pretending to believe me, which was really nice of her. "I wish I was more like you, but sometimes I just get so mad."

"What do you mean?"

She stared at me, but probably only because she was

painting me. "I don't know, Charlie Joe. As soon as I realized he was the kid who made me fall in the mud puddle in kindergarten, it was like I didn't even have control of myself. I had to go out there and do something about it." She shook her head. "One of these days I'll probably get myself in real trouble."

"I don't know what you're talking about," I said. "All you're doing is sticking up for yourself, which is pretty awesome, I think." Wow, that came out dorky.

But she just smiled back at me. "You're awesome, too."

Wow. This girl was really something. Ten minutes ago I was feeling like the biggest coward in the world, and now she was making me feel all warm and funny inside.

And that's when it hit me: Was something happening here with a girl that was non-Hannah-related?

But Mrs. Massey ruined the mood by clapping her hands. "Okay, Zoe, Charlie Joe, that's enough chitchat, we're here to work."

"You guys can call me Byron, if it helps with your painting."

Zoe giggled. "That's silly. Your name is perfect. You're totally a Charlie Joe."

"I shall call you Charlie Joe as well, since it is your name," Mrs. Massey announced. "And I will thank YOU to not call me a 'guy.' "

And I sat, and they painted.

Charlie Joe's Tip #12

SOMETIMES EXTRA CREDIT JUST ISN'T WORTH IT.

There's a fine line between getting extra credit and having no life.

Don't cross it.

Here are a few sure signs you're doing too much extra credit:

1. *You forget to eat dessert.*
2. *You don't use up your maximum allowed text messages for the month.*
3. *You haven't thought about Hannah Spivero for six straight hours.*
4. *The screen on your television is cold.*
5. *Teachers actually smile when they see you coming.*

"That is unbelievable," Jake said, as I finished telling him the Zoe-Pete story. "Pete must have been freaking out."

"I don't think I've ever seen him scared like that," I said. If I blocked out the part about me freezing up, I could really enjoy the memory.

Jake was over at my house, helping me with Science and Spanish. Since my friends had started helping me study, I was doing awesome. It's not just that they were so smart, it's also that they kind of guilted me into caring. If they were going to help me, the least I could do was accept their help, right? And if I ever felt like slacking off, all I had to do was look at the brochure of Camp Rituhbukkee. Seeing a picture of a bunch of kids reading in a sweaty cabin always did the trick.

In any event, with Jake, Katie, and Nareem's help, I was turning into a total brainiac. I know what you're thinking. Charlie Joe Jackson, brainiac? I didn't believe it myself.

But Jake wasn't that interested in studying that day. "I need to talk to you about Hannah."

Oh boy. She was dumping him. I knew this day would come. It was only a matter of time before the world's most perfect creature realized that she was dating a boy with glasses.

"What's up?"

"She getting too clingy," he said.

I thought maybe I had wax in my ears. "Did you say 'clingy'?"

"Yeah," Jake nodded. "Don't get me wrong, she's totally completely great and everything, and I'm so lucky to have her, but every once in a while I kind of feel like she's suffocating me. That day with the Summer Planning Committee was like the first time in forever that we hung out with other people, and she didn't even want to go at first."

I was too shocked to say anything, so he went on. "I thought at our age, being boyfriend and girlfriend was more about texting and stuff, but she wants to be together like all the time."

I was confused. "But you're over here right now, helping me study."

"This doesn't count, because it's homework-related. And besides, our parents wouldn't let us hang out during the week anyway. But on the weekends, it seems like Hannah and I are together all the time. And sometimes I want to do other things, you know, fun things like reading and relaxing and hanging out with friends and things like that."

I wanted to point out that reading was the opposite of a fun thing, but decided not to.

"Oh, yeah, I totally get it," I said. "That happens with me

all the time, too. Once a girl gets her hooks in you, man, forget it." I had no idea what I was talking about, but I'm pretty sure Jake didn't realize that, or didn't care, or both.

"So what should I do?" he asked.

I had to come up with something. Here he was, teaching me all about geometric equations and how to say, "take out the trash" in Spanish. The least I could do was give him a little relationship advice. Even if I'd never exactly had a relationship.

"Well, what if you guys started hanging around with your friends more? Then maybe after a while, she'd be okay with you hanging out with us by yourself, without her, every once in a while."

Jake scrunched up his eyes, the way he does when he's thinking about something. "It might be weird, me and her and my friends. What would we do?"

"I don't know, like go to the movies or something. I'll go to the movies with you guys if you want."

"You?"

He looked at me suspiciously. He knew how I felt about Hannah, and he wasn't sure he wanted to go down that road.

"Dude, I'm totally over Hannah," I said. "I've moved on. In fact, you know Zoe, the girl I was just telling you about, who kicked the soccer ball at Pete? I think she might like me. Maybe she can come, too. It'll be like a double date." I learned about double dates from my sister Megan. Actually, anything I knew at all about dating and stuff came from Megan.

Jake looked skeptical. "I don't know. I don't think Hannah will go for it."

"Let me talk to her," I said, getting kind of excited about the idea. "I'm sure I can talk her into it." As I waited for Jake's answer, I pictured being at the movies with Hannah on one side of me, and Zoe on the other. My heart started beating kind of fast.

Finally Jake nodded. "Okay. Why not? Let's try it. As long as Zoe goes, too."

We went back to studying, but for some reason I wasn't able to concentrate very well.

WEDNESDAY

Right after I woke up, I texted Hannah: I NEED TO TALK TO YOU TODAY.

Then I lay in bed, staring at my phone for five minutes—five brutally long minutes—until she finally texted back: WHY?

IT'S ABOUT JAKE.

That got her attention. Ten seconds later: OK! AFTER SCHOOL?

I got in the shower without responding, knowing she would be sitting there, waiting impatiently. That was fun.

Downstairs, eating cereal, I finally responded: CAN'T. SGC.

Six seconds later: BOO! WHEN?

"Boo?" I mumbled to myself. "Who says 'boo'?"

Mom poured herself some coffee. "Do you have to text every single minute of every hour of every day?" she asked.

"Yes, we do," Megan answered, on behalf of both of us.

I looked at my dad, who was staring at his laptop as usual,

wearing nothing but a business shirt and boxer shorts.

"What about him?" I said to my mom. "He's way worse than us."

"I gave up on Dad a long time ago," she said.

We all watched him, alone in his e-mail world.

"Honey, I'm pregnant," my mom said. No reaction.

"Dad, I'm a drug addict," Megan said. No reaction.

"Dad, I'm a pregnant drug addict," I said. No reaction.

Finally he looked up.

So sad.

MEET END OF LUNCH? I texted Hannah.

Her: K. IS JAKE MAD ABOUT SOMETHING? NERVOUS HAHA!

Me: NO, NOT MAD.

Her: PHEW! GTG ☺

Wow! That was an intense exchange with Hannah. I put my phone away, feeling elated and bummed out at the same time.

I had received maybe a thousand texts from Hannah in my life, and never once had she included an exclamation point. Now all of a sudden, in just five texts she writes me about Jake, there are four exclamation points. Plus a happy face.

Life is so unfair sometimes.

I sat at lunch with Timmy, Katie, and Nareem, but I had one eye on the next table over, where Hannah was eating with Eliza and the Elizettes.

"You shouldn't stare over there in such a conspicuous fashion," Nareem said.

"And don't be so obvious about it, either," Timmy added.

"I'm not staring," I insisted. "It's just that I have to talk to Hannah after lunch, and I want to make sure we have time."

"Talk about what?" asked Katie.

"I can't really talk about it."

Nareem, Timmy, and Katie all looked at each other. Then they waited. They knew I'd be unable to resist. They were right.

"Jake is worried that Hannah is getting too clingy," I said.

"You probably shouldn't have told us that," Katie said.

Timmy nodded. "Yeah, that sounds private."

"You guys are so annoying," I said.

"Be careful with what you say to Hannah," Nareem advised. "From what Katie tells me, she is in a rather delicate

emotional state about Jake, and you don't want to push her so far that she responds by acting in an irrational manner."

"She's getting up," Timmy reported. We all looked. Hannah was, in fact, getting up. She said good-bye to Eliza and the Elizettes and headed straight for me.

Except for the fact that she was coming to talk about her boyfriend who wasn't me, this was the moment I'd been waiting for my whole life.

We went to an empty table.

"So what's up with Jake?"

Hannah wanted to get right down to business. Fine with me.

"Well, we were wondering if you wanted to go to the movies with us."

She laughed.

"No, I'm serious," I said. "Me and you and Jake and maybe one or two other kids."

Hannah scratched her head. "Wait, what? I don't get it. You said you wanted to talk to me about Jake. What does going to the movies have to do with it?"

"It was his idea." Which wasn't entirely technically true.

She squinted at me. "What do you mean it was his idea?"

"Well, he kind of misses hanging around with his friends, so we thought maybe it would be fun to all do something together."

Oops.

I wasn't supposed to say that part, but I couldn't help it—it just slipped out. I swear.

Hannah's eyes went wide, like she'd seen a ghost.

She punched me in the arm, kind of hard. "I thought you said it wasn't bad! You texted me it wasn't bad!"

"Ow," I answered.

Hannah leaned in closer. "What are you telling me?" she whispered. "Does he want to break up with me?"

"Definitely not," I answered quickly, in case another punch was coming. "He still totally likes you. But like I said, he misses his friends, and I think he just wants to make sure that you guys still do stuff besides only hang out with each other."

"We almost never hang out," Hannah insisted.

"Well, he thinks you do," I insisted back, unhelpfully.

Hannah took out a tissue. Wow, was she going to cry over Jake? I imagined her crying over *me*. What a moment that would be. What a triumph. What a—

"So you think maybe a bunch of us should go to the movies together?" she asked, interrupting my private moment. "Who's a bunch of us?"

Now we were getting to the good part.

"Well, I thought it could be you and Jake and me and Zoe."

I could swear she looked a little hurt for a split second, but maybe I was imagining it.

"You like her? I knew it!"

"I don't know. Maybe. I've gotten to know her a little in my extra-credit art project and she's really cool."

"Yeah, I heard what happened with her and Pete. She sounds a little crazy."

"She's not crazy. She's just kind of fearless."

Hannah took a deep breath. "So my boyfriend is annoyed because I want to be with him too much, and the one guy who's liked me forever suddenly gets a new girlfriend. This has been a great little chat, Charlie Joe, thanks."

"She's not my girlfriend."

"But she will be, right?"

So she *was* a little jealous! I couldn't believe it.

Then, as if the conversation hadn't been weird enough, Mr. Twipple, the Drama teacher, stopped by our table.

"Well, Mr. Jackson? Have you thought any more about our conversation? Will you be joining us in the school play this year?"

"Um, actually I'm not sure. I hadn't really thought about it that much yet."

Mr. Twipple took a bite out of his apple. "Well, sign-ups are going on right now, so don't dawdle." He started to walk away.

Suddenly Hannah stood up. "He's going to audition, and so am I!"

Mr. Twipple turned around. "And you are . . . ?"

Hannah walked over and shook his hand. "I'm Hannah Spivero, and I've always wanted to try acting. And Charlie Joe and I have talked about it, and we're both going to try out for the school play this year."

I was too shocked to move.

"Well, that's terrific news!" said Mr. Twipple. "We can always use some new blood. I'll look forward to seeing you both."

I stared at Hannah. "What was that about?"

She smiled, back to her usual happy self.

"You and me, spending quality time together! Isn't that awesome? Isn't that what you've always wanted?"

She was right. It was the moment I'd been dreaming of practically my whole life.

But for some reason it wasn't awesome. It was confusing.

What was happening to me?

After school, I had my first SGC meeting. When I walked in, the first thing I noticed was Katie Friedman.

"What are you doing here?!" I asked her.

"I'm in the SGC," she answered.

"For real?

"There's a lot you don't know about me," Katie said, "which is why I'm so endlessly fascinating."

I was trying to decide if she was being serious or not when Mr. Radonski marched into the room.

"Let's get started," Mr. Radonski barked. "For those of you who are new to our organization, we run a tight ship here. We start on time, we conduct our business, we end on time." He pointed at a tiny woman sitting next to him, pecking away at a laptop. "As usual, Mrs. Chelton will be taking the minutes."

We were sitting in the middle of the gym on a bunch of folding chairs. My eyes kept drifting up to the ceiling, where a bunch of balls were stuck in the netting. I wondered how long those balls had been up there. Probably some of them for like fifty years.

"Stop staring into space," Katie whispered.

"Look at all those balls up there," I whispered back.

There were nine students on the SGC, plus the two teachers. The only kids I knew personally were Katie and Nareem. I'd started to notice that Nareem seemed to go everywhere Katie went.

Mr. Radonski banged a hammer down on the table, like he was some sort of judge. "First, let's welcome our new member. Charlie Joe Jackson has decided to join SGC, which may be a shock to some of you. It certainly was to me. But let's give him the benefit of the doubt. For now." Everyone clapped for about half a second.

He picked up a clipboard. "And now to business."

A skinny freckle-faced kid raised his hand. Mr. Radonski nodded. "Yes, Richard?"

Freckly Richard stood up. "I'd like to remind the council that at last Friday's meeting, I brought up the idea of making the break after lunch two minutes longer, to give students an opportunity to put their lunch materials away and still get to class on time." Richard looked nervously at Mr. Radonski. "You had asked that we table the issue until today, so I'm just reminding you that I'd still like to discuss it."

Mr. Radonski looked at his notes. "That's terrific, Richard, your idea is certainly worth discussing, but I'm afraid today's agenda is extremely full. My guess is that we won't be able to get to it, unfortunately."

Richard looked at Mrs. Chelton, who kept staring at her computer. He shrugged and sat down, and I suddenly realized how this whole thing worked. The Student Government Council was just an excuse for Mr. Radonski to boss a few kids around two times a week after school.

I glanced at Katie. "Is it always like this?"

She glanced back. "Just wait."

***

As the meeting went on, Mr. Radonski managed to reject Katie's idea to use smaller school buses since the big ones were never more than half full ("too complicated"), to ignore another girl Tonya's request to keep the library open after school ("staffing issues"), and to laugh at Nareem's suggestion that certain students be allowed to attend certain classes at the high school ("hard to manage").

This was clearly not a government. This was a dictatorship. I was pretty sure it wouldn't help me get an A, but I had to do something, so I raised my hand. "I have an idea."

Mr. Radonski snorted. "This I gotta hear."

I stood up. "I think we should elect a president of the SGC."

Everyone started talking at once.

"Quiet!" said Mr. Radonski unquietly. He looked at me. "And why do you think that? This is a democracy. Having a president would make one of us more powerful than the others." Apparently he hadn't been listening to himself for the past hour.

“I still think we should have a president, and I think it should be one of the students. I nominate Nareem Ramdal.”

Nareem coughed and spit out some water.

“I second the motion,” said Katie.

“I third it,” said some kid who had been looking at his reflection in the window the whole time.

Mr. Radonski threw down his clipboard. “This is insane.” He looked at Mrs. Chelton. “Please set these children straight.”

Mrs. Chelton looked up from her computer for the first time all day.

“I fourth it,” she said.

For the next fifteen minutes, while Mr. Radonski just sat there like a big sourpuss, we actually got some things done. Nareem got us all to agree that we would put forward the idea of smaller school buses to the principal, Mrs. Sleep, on Friday, when she would be joining the meeting for her monthly visit. And we decided that Richard's idea about a longer break after lunch was not going to work, since it would probably take time away from recess.

Then, with about two minutes left in the meeting, Mr. Radonski stood up. "I'd like to bring up a topic."

"Here we go again," Katie muttered under her breath.

"Here what goes again?" I asked.

"The time has come once and for all for Ambidexterity Week," Mr. Radonski announced. "You all know this is a pet project of mine, and I've been very patient about it. But now that we have an SGC president, I feel that the time is right to bring it up again." He looked at Nareem. "Mr. Ramdal, would you mind if I took the floor for just a moment?"

"You have the floor," Nareem answered, sounding pretty presidential, actually.

Mr. Radonski stuck out his chest, the way he always did when he wanted to seem important. "Most of you know how passionately I feel about the subject of ambidexterity. It is a scandal that our children have such poor use of their weaker hands and feet. We are way behind the rest of the world in that regard. We need to fix that immediately, and there is no better way to start the process than by instituting our first annual Ambidexterity Week."

I raised my hand. "I don't understand. We already do Opposite-Hand Thursdays."

Mr. Radonski took a deep breath, like he was trying to remain calm. He pointed at the bruise on his forehead. "You of all people, Jackson, should understand why this is important. Ambidexterity Week is the key to the future of our children. It is a week in which all the students of this school would be required to do everything with their opposite hand or opposite foot."

"Everything?"

"Yes, everything. From writing papers to shooting baskets to kicking balls. Even playing badminton. Everything."

I looked at Katie. She rolled her eyes. "Don't ask."

Mr. Radonski turned to Nareem. "Mr. Ramdal, would you please put the motion to a vote? I would like to bring it up with Mrs. Sleep this Friday, but I need the support of the students on this council."

Nareem cleared his throat. "All in favor of bringing up

the idea of Ambidexterity Week to Mrs. Sleep on Friday, raise your hand."

Mr. Radonski raised his hand. Then he glared his way around the room, until he got five hands up. He glared at Nareem, and his hand went up. He glared at Katie, and after about five seconds, her hand went up.

"Really?" I said to her.

"I just want more fuel-efficient school buses," she said back.

Mr. Radonski turned to me. I didn't know what to do. Ambidexterity Week was the dumbest idea I'd ever heard in my life.

But then again, it would only last a week. Camp Rituhbukkee would last all summer.

I raised my hand.

Then I took it down and raised my other hand. My left hand. My weak hand.

"It's never too early to start practicing," I said.

"Can I ask you something?" I said to Katie, as we waited for our moms to pick us up. "What made you join SGC? I know you're into studying people and stuff like that, but it's like a total waste of time."

"I don't think so," she said.

"Really? Radonski's crazy. He's like a total Nazi."

"That's what makes the group dynamic so fascinating."

Katie had this habit every once in a while of saying something way too smart for me.

"I don't know what a group dynamic is."

"Well, it's how people act when they get in a group. They tend to all act the same way. Especially if someone takes charge. Suddenly there's one leader, and everyone else is a follower. And nobody even notices it until something changes the group dynamic."

I thought about that for a second, until my head started to hurt.

"Like today, when you came in, it changed the group dynamic," Katie continued. "But only for a little while. Mr. Radonski wasn't sure how to react by having his leadership challenged, but then he realized that he could actually use it to his advantage. And we all fell into line and became his followers again." She sighed. "Am I like totally boring you?"

I shook my head. "Just because you're smart doesn't mean you're boring."

"Thanks, Charlie Joe."

"At least not this time," I added.

Katie punched me in the arm, just as her mom pulled up. She hopped in the car, then she stuck her head out the window.

"By the way, there are exactly forty-six balls stuck in the net above the gym. I've counted them lots of times."

Then she stuck her head back in and was gone.

Charlie Joe's Tip #13

THERE'S SUCH A THING AS TOO MUCH EXTRA CREDIT.

In Tip #5, I explained that you have to like a teacher in order for them to like you. But if you like them too much, they'll hate you. And that's bad.

So don't overdo it on your extra credit project. Don't show up in your teacher's classroom all the time, or ask them questions in the cafeteria line, or stay after school every day to work on your project. If you do that, it will backfire. Because then the teacher won't have any more free time to call his wife or surf the Internet, and they'll blame you for it.

Nobody likes a teacher's pet.

Especially teachers.

THURSDAY

After school, I changed into my costume for the last day of posing. But when I got back to the studio, Zoe was crying, and Mrs. Massey was pacing back and forth, talking on the phone.

I ran over to them. "What's going on?"

Zoe pointed at her easel. I looked, and suddenly felt a little sick.

Her painting had been splashed with red paint.

It was completely destroyed.

I stood there in shock, not able to speak. I wouldn't have known what to say anyway.

"I can't believe him," Zoe said.

"Who?" I managed to ask.

"Who do you think?" she snapped, and I suddenly realized she was talking about Pete.

"He wouldn't do something like this," I said. But deep down, I knew maybe he would. And that made me feel lousy. Even though Pete was totally obnoxious, I still considered him my friend, and the idea that a friend of mine would ruin Zoe's painting was pretty messed up.

Mrs. Massey hung up the phone. "Charlie Joe, I don't think we'll be needing you today." She turned to Zoe. "That was school security. There's no way we'll be able to prove anything, unfortunately. I'm not sure there's a thing we can do about it."

I wanted so badly to help Zoe, but I felt that helpless, frozen feeling rising up inside me again. This time, though, I wasn't going to let it happen.

"I'll be right back," I said.

With Mrs. Massey and Zoe staring at me, I ran out of the room, out of the school, down to the soccer field, and right up to Pete Milano. My heart was pounding, but I tried to ignore it.

"Who do you think you are?" I screamed at Pete. "You need to pay for what you did!"

He looked at me, and actually looked a little scared. I

think he thought that any kid who would run up and scream at him while wearing a red vest and tiny green shorts had to be even crazier than he was.

"What are you talking about?"

I poked my finger in his chest. "You have committed a dastardly act of cowardice and must make amends immediately!"

Wow. I may have been taking this whole Byron Chillingsworth a little too far. I didn't even know I *knew* the words *dastardly* and *amends*.

"Charlie Joe, cut the crap," Pete said.

"You cut the crap!" I yelled, but I'd barely gotten the words out of my mouth, when Pete grabbed my little checkered jacket and put it on.

"Hey, look at me!" he announced to his teammates. "I'm little Dweeby McDorkenton!"

Everybody started cracking up. I suddenly felt a little less heroic. Pete took off with my jacket, and I ran after him. He started running around in circles, holding the jacket over his head, with me chasing him. The soccer kids gathered around, watching and pointing. But I wasn't going to give up, not this time.

Until I heard a sickening *RRRIIIIPPP!*

Pete stopped. I stopped. Everything stopped. I looked down, expecting the worst.

Yup. My little green shorts had ripped all the way down the back.

You could have heard the laughter in Alaska.

"Little Lord McDorkenton's shorts ripped!" Pete screamed, stating the obvious.

Everyone howled, and it was probably the most embarrassing moment of my entire life, but somehow I managed to say, "How could you do that to her painting?"

Pete poked me in the chest. "I didn't touch her freakin' painting, you little pantsless dweeb!"

Mr. Betts, the soccer coach, came running over. "Now what?" Right behind him were Zoe and Mrs. Massey. Zoe was still crying a little bit. She looked at me and tried to smile.

Mrs. Massey stared at Pete. "We're not leaving until you admit you destroyed that painting."

"Admit what you did," Zoe said very quietly, but in a voice that made everyone shut up and take notice. What was it about her? How did she do that so easily?

"Pete, is this true?" Mr. Betts said. "Did you do what they're saying you did?"

Everyone stared at Pete. Even his own teammates seemed like they were waiting for Pete to come clean. He looked around wildly and started blinking really fast.

Finally Mrs. Massey went over to him and put her hand on his shoulder. "Tell the truth, Peter," she said. "Please."

"WHATEVER!" Pete yelled. "Fine! I didn't mean to do it. I was just going to sign my name in the corner, really tiny, like as a joke. But when I squeezed the tube of paint there was this big rip in the side and it spilled all over everything." He sat on the ground, suddenly looking like he was about to cry. "And when I tried to wipe it off, it got worse. I'm really, really sorry."

Zoe stared at him. "What else are you sorry about?"

Pete took the deepest breath I've ever seen in my life.

"I shouldn't have dropped you in the mud puddle in kindergarten. That was stupid." He looked up at her. "I'm really, really sorry about that, too."

Everyone stood there, waiting for Zoe's reaction. Would she scream at him? Would she smack him? Would she kick another soccer ball at his you-know-what?

She didn't do any of those things.

Instead, she actually smiled a little. "Thank you for apologizing. It's okay. The same thing happened to me the other day. I don't know what it is about that darn tube of red paint." Then she stuck out her hand. "I forgive you."

Pete's blinking slowed down to a human level. "You do?"

"Yes. Just be nice from now on. Is it a deal?"

He smiled the biggest smile I'd ever seen. "Deal, totally!"

"And don't ever push someone into a mud puddle again," Zoe said. "That's really, really not nice at all."

Pete looked at the ground. "I know."

They shook hands, and Mr. Betts blew his whistle. "Well, that's a happy ending. Now everybody get back to work!"

As all the soccer players ran onto the field, I headed

back inside. Halfway up the hill, I felt a hand on my shoulder. It was Zoe.

"Thank you, Charlie Joe."

"For what?"

"For being brave."

I shook my head. "You're just being nice. I wasn't being brave. I tried to get Pete to admit what he did but all I ended up doing was splitting my pants."

Zoe stopped and turned to look at me. "What you did—trying to help someone else, to make them feel better—that's the bravest thing in the whole world."

I thought about that for a second. Was she right? I decided to give her the benefit of the doubt.

"Thanks, I guess."

"No, thank YOU," Zoe said.

"You're welcome." Then before I knew it I blurted out, "Um, hey, do you want to go to the movies with me?"

She stopped walking for a split second, and then started again. "I'll have to ask my parents."

"Uh-oh," I said nervously. Some parents were really strict.

She stopped again, and gave me one of those smiles. "Would they say no to the boy who defended my honor?"

Then she kissed me on the cheek and ran up the hill.

I watched her go, touching my cheek and absorbing an important lesson:

Be brave—or at least, try to be brave—and good things can happen.

Back in the studio, we stared at Zoe's painting for about ten minutes.

"I should just throw it out," Zoe said.

"We never throw anything out," Mrs. Massey said. "It is still a piece of art. It will always be a piece of art."

That gave me an idea.

"Hey, did I ever tell you about this painting my parents have hanging over our fireplace?" I asked Mrs. Massey. "I used to think it was the ugliest thing I'd ever seen, until my dad told me it was worth like three thousand dollars."

They looked at me, listening.

"It looks like a combination of a bathtub, a shoe, and a French fry. My dad's college roommate painted it, so we bought it from him as a favor. Then the guy becomes like this big-deal artist." I picked up Zoe's painting. "So you never know, this baby could be worth a lot of money one day."

Zoe tried to laugh. "That's sweet, Charlie Joe."

I blushed. At least I think I did. The problem with blushing is that you can never be sure you're blushing because you can't see it. But you can feel it. Yeah, I was blushing.

I went back to posing, so Mrs. Massey could finish her painting. It came out really good. Zoe spent the rest of the time trying to scrape off some of the red paint, but it didn't really work, and she just ended up making it all hard and crusty. Finally, she just gave up and stared out the window.

After a while, there was a knock on the door. "Yoo-hoo!"

My mom came into the room, a big smile as always. "I had to see for myself what was going on in here!"

"Mrs. Jackson, how nice to see you," said Mrs. Massey.

My mom looked at Mrs. Massey's painting. "That's just wonderful!"

Mrs. Massey beamed. "Thank you so much. Your son has been a huge help. He's been a fine foxhunter for us this past week."

"I always knew he belonged in suspenders and hot pants," Mom said. Then she saw Zoe at the window. "And who's this?"

"This is my granddaughter Zoe," said Mrs. Massey.

"She's a great painter, too." I said. "And we're going to the movies."

"Good to know," my mom said. "Where's your painting, Zoe?"

Zoe shrugged sadly.

I pointed. "It's over there. Isn't it awesome?"

My mom examined the damaged painting and glanced back at Zoe, who was still staring out the window.

Then my mom looked at me, and I looked at her, and we had one of those classic mother-son moments where she knew exactly what I wanted her to do. (I love it when that happens.)

"It's a completely awesome painting," my mom said. "Somehow you managed to combine a painting of a fox-hunter with an artistic statement about how hunting is both a sport of kings and an act of violence all at the same time." Then she ran her hand over the hard and crusty part. "And this texture is really terrific."

Zoe got up from the window and stood next to my mom, looking at her own painting. I joined them.

"I just told Zoe that it would probably be worth a lot of money some day," I said. "Somebody would be really smart to buy it."

My mom turned to Zoe. "Well, I'm smart! I would like to buy this painting."

Zoe blinked. "You would?"

My mom got out her purse. "I would. Does twenty-five dollars seem fair?"

"You're a professional artist!" Mrs. Massey exclaimed to Zoe, clapping her hands.

Zoe looked at her painting, as if for the first time. "I guess it is pretty cool, huh?"

As my mom paid Zoe, Mrs. Massey squeezed my arm.

"You done good, kid," she whispered. "You done real good."

"This extra credit project was really interesting," I said, saying good-bye to Mrs. Massey.

She hugged me. "Want to do it again sometime?"

"I'll get back to you on that," I said, and she laughed.

Then I turned to Zoe. "I'll text you."

She didn't say anything. She just kissed my cheek, for the second time in twenty minutes.

Not that I was keeping track or anything.

Phew.

My A in Art seemed pretty locked up.

But even though one extra-credit assignment was done, there was no time to congratulate myself. The SGC meeting with the principal was the next day, and I had no idea what was going to happen. All I knew was that I needed to figure out a way to get an A out of Mr. Radonski.

Which wouldn't be easy if he presented his ambidexterity plan and Mrs. Sleep realized he was a complete crazypants.

Charlie Joe's Tip #14

IN GENERAL, TRY TO DO ONE EXTRA CREDIT PROJECT AT A TIME.

It's bad enough that you have to take Math, Science, English, Social Studies, and a foreign language all at the same time. But that's how school works, and unfortunately there's nothing you can do about it.

But extra credit is under your control. You make the rules. And your number one rule should be, only do one extra credit project at a time. You have enough to do with homework and chores and stuff, and you need to make sure there's plenty of time left over for playing video games, watching TV, and listening to music, preferably all three at the same time.

Only do a lot of extra credit projects at the same time if you have absolutely no choice. Like, for example, to get out of going to summer reading camp.

FRIDAY

Jake cornered me by the slide at recess.

"Hannah just told me you two are trying out for the school play together."

I wondered why she had waited so long to tell him. She probably changed her mind about doing the play like five times. Girls do that.

"Well, not exactly together. But yeah, I guess we're both trying out."

Jake looked at me long and hard. "Whose idea was that?"

"Totally hers!" I said. "But she's doing it to make you happy. Think about it. You said she was clingy. You thought she was taking up too much of your time. So now she's doing something else, so you can hang out with your friends and read and do things like that. It's perfect."

"I agree, it is perfect. For her. Why are you doing it?"

"Extra credit, remember?"

Jake banged his hand on the slide angrily, which was weird, since he basically never got mad. "Yeah, I remember. I just don't get why you have to try out for the play.

It's Drama class, for crying out loud! It's like the easiest A in the school! Why can't you just sit there nicely? Why do you always have to talk to the teachers like you're another teacher, and not one of their students? Why can't you just act like a normal well-behaved kid?"

It was a fair question, and I didn't really have an answer. I guess I just never realized it was an option.

Charlie Joe's Tip #15

NEVER DO EXTRA CREDIT ON AN EMPTY STOMACH.

Everyone knows that the body needs nourishment to grow.

But not everybody knows that the brain needs nourishment to be smart.

And if you're staying after school to do an extra-credit project, that means you're not going to be home for your usual snack of cookies, cereal, and perhaps a medium- to large-sized bowl of ice cream.

So make sure your mom or dad gives you plenty of extra lunch money, if at all possible.

Then, with that extra money, make sure you buy cookies, pudding, and ice cream sandwiches.

(Tip #15a: The brain does not consider vegetables to be nourishment. Except for asparagus. For some weird reason I love asparagus, so it gets a pass.)

46

The monthly SGC meeting with Mrs. Sleep was a big deal. It was held in a big conference room that was connected to her office. There was a long table, with lots of comfy chairs. It would have been very easy to take a nap in one of those chairs.

They also served cookies and milk, which was a nice touch.

When I got there, Nareem was already sitting with Richard, the freckly kid. Nareem had a gavel, one of those things a judge bangs when he wants attention.

I immediately helped myself to four Oreo cookies.

"You're not supposed to eat until Mrs. Sleep gets here," freckly Richard whispered.

"Oops," I said, shoving them in my mouth. "Foo fate."

One by one, the group wandered in. Mrs. Chelton came in and immediately opened her laptop and started typing, even though the meeting hadn't started yet. Katie saw me with my mouth full and asked me why I was such a doofus, even though I could tell she wanted a cookie.

Eventually, the only people who weren't there yet were Mr. Radonski and Mrs. Sleep.

For about five minutes, we all just looked at each other and wondered what to do. Finally Nareem spoke up.

"As the president of SGC, I move to postpone today's meeting unless the principal arrives in the next several minutes. She has probably been called away to other pressing business, and I'm sure most of us could be using this time wisely. I'm sure we all have homework to do, for example."

"I don't," said a kid with long hair who probably joined the SGC to try and turn the school into a skateboard park.

"Where's Mr. Radonski?" asked Katie. "He's never late."

"HERE I AM!" came a yell from down the hall. Two seconds later, Mr. Radonski came running into the room, out of breath and carrying a huge box.

He threw the box on the table. "Go ahead, open it!" he said to the room.

Nobody took him up on his offer.

"Fine," Mr. Radonski said, sitting down. "It's better as a surprise anyway."

"What's in it?" asked Richard. "Is it food?"

"No, it's not food," Mr. Radonski hissed.

"That's disappointing," said a booming voice behind us. "I love food." We all turned around, and Mrs. Sleep was standing in the doorway, taller than ever, her huge glasses sitting on the tip of her nose. She eyed the box. "What *is* in it then?"

"It's a surprise!" Mr. Radonski answered.

Mrs. Sleep came into the room and took her seat at the head of the table. "So sorry I'm late," she announced. "I was dealing with a mother who wants to know why her child wasn't recommended for honors math in high school." She chuckled. "Everyone thinks their child is a genius."

"Katie is a genius," I volunteered.

Katie slid down in her chair. Everyone looked at me like I was crazy. Nareem tried not to laugh.

Mrs. Sleep looked at me over her glasses. "Thank you for that insight, Charles Joseph. When did you join the SGC?"

"This week."

"And may I ask why?"

I hesitated, and then decided to go with the truth. "Because Mr. Radonski thought I had a lot of ideas." Which *was* the truth. Just not the whole truth.

"Well, good for you," Mrs. Sleep said. "Now, what business are we attending to today?" She looked at the box again. "Will someone please tell me what this is about?"

Mr. Radonski stood up and nodded at Nareem. "Mr. Ramdal, if I may have the floor?" Then he turned to Mrs. Sleep. "He's been elected president."

Nareem seemed to have lost his presidential ability to speak, so he just nodded.

Mr. Radonski stood up. "You all know it's been a dream of mine to teach these kids how to use their weaker hands and feet. That's why we do Opposite-Hand Thursdays in Gym. Well, now the time has come to take it up a notch. The committee and I propose to institute an annual week here at school where the students are ONLY allowed to use their opposite limbs."

Then he opened the box. It was filled with shirts. He took one out and held it up, like the way Mufasa holds up Simba at the beginning of *The Lion King*.

AMBIDEXTERITY WEEK, it said on the front.

He turned it around.

A WEEK LONG. TO MAKE THE WEAK STRONG, it said on the back.

He pulled the shirt on over his shirt and tie, which looked pretty wrong.

"A week long, to make the weak strong!" he announced, in case some of us couldn't read.

No one said anything.

Mr. Radonski waited for Mrs. Sleep to tell him what a

great idea it was, but instead, she just sat there and stared at him.

"Ambidexterity Week, is that what you said?" she asked.

"Yes, ma'am," he answered.

More silence.

Mr. Radonski sat back down. "It would be for writing and sports and stuff," he added, a little less confidently.

Mrs. Sleep stared some more, and then finally gave a tiny shake of her huge head.

"Mr. Radonski. The staff has heard you talk about ambidexterity for years, and we've put up with it, because your passion is indeed admirable. But this is going way too far, even for you. These are middle school children! It's hard enough to teach them how to write well with their good hand, or throw a ball accurately. The idea of having them use their opposite limbs for all activities for an entire week is dangerously impractical."

Mr. Radonski slumped in his seat.

Nobody said anything. I saw Mr. Radonski's ears burning. I saw my A in Gym going up in smoke. I saw a summer of reading, writing, and sleeping in a cabin with lots of kids wearing glasses.

I had to do something.

I stood up. “I think it’s a great idea.”

For the second time in about three minutes, everybody looked at me like I was crazy.

Mr. Radonski took his head out of his hands. “You do?”

I went over to the blackboard. “I will write my name with my right hand.”

And I wrote CHARLIE JOE JACKSON.

“Now I will write my name with my left hand.”

And I wrote Wj9iəflloƒH.

“See?” I said. “My left hand is hopeless. I think the idea of making kids more ambidextrous makes total sense.”

"But why would you ever need to write with your left hand?" Nareem asked.

"There are tons of reasons," I said, trying to think of one.

"You could lose your right hand in an accident," Katie offered, coming to my rescue as usual.

"Or in a war," said the long-haired skateboard kid.

"Or your right hand could fall asleep and never wake up and then it would just be numb forever," said Richard.

Mrs. Chelton looked up from her laptop. "This is a cheerful conversation."

"That will do," Mrs. Sleep declared, shutting everybody up. "I'm sorry, but we simply cannot ask the children to spend an entire week writing and taking tests and doing homework with their opposite hand." She looked directly at Mr. Radonski. "I think perhaps we should discuss this privately after the meeting."

Uh-oh. This was not going well. I had to do something, and I had to do it fast.

Suddenly I remembered I had my baseball glove and ball in my backpack, because I had practice after school. I pulled them out, walked over to Mrs. Sleep, and handed her the glove. "Would you put this on, please?" I asked.

By this point, people had stopped looking at me like I was crazy.

Now they were looking at me like I was on death row.

But Mrs. Sleep was an interesting person. She was

grumpy, she was crabby, she was definitely scary at times, but she was very old-fashioned. And that meant she lived by a strict code: Students came first. If a student asked her to do something, and the student wasn't misbehaving or being naughty, she would do it.

So she put on the baseball glove.

I went around to the other side of the big table, and started telling the most important story of my life. Some of it was even true.

"When I was a little kid, I wanted to be a pitcher when I grew up," I said. "I know that sounds like every other kid, but I was really serious. I was like, obsessed. To the point where it was all I could think about for a while."

I did always love baseball, but I thought about a lot of other things too, like chocolate and Hannah Spivero.

"One day, I looked up how hard it was to become a professional baseball pitcher," I continued. "The odds were like .0000001 percent. But you know what the interesting thing was? It was a lot easier for a lefty than a righty."

Katie helped herself to an Oreo, which looked delicious. But this was no time for distractions.

"So I decided I would become a lefty. I practiced throwing a ball with my left hand for hours every day. My dream was to pitch left-handed in a little league game."

I put the baseball on the table.

"It was the third grade championship game. We needed

one more out. James Edwards, the best hitter on the other team, was coming up. The kid we had pitching was getting tired, so the coach pointed at me. I went out to the mound. I took my warm-up pitches right-handed. Then, when James came up, took my glove off and pitched my last warm-up pitch left-handed. When people saw me, they went wild. James pointed at me, complaining, like it was illegal to switch hands. But of course it isn't. It's perfectly legal. It's just never done, because no one is ambidextrous."

People were really listening now. I paused for dramatic effect.

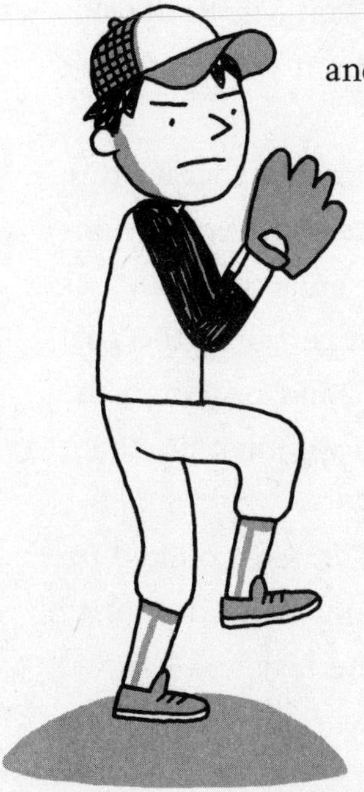

"I struck James out in three pitches, and we were little league champions."

A cheer went up around the room. Nareem and Freckly Richard high-fived each other. Even the skateboard kid seemed impressed. Mr. Radonski banged his hands on the table happily. And I think I might have seen Mrs. Sleep wipe a tear from her eye.

Katie was the only one who wasn't overcome by the moment. In fact, she was shaking her head at me. Luckily I was the only one who noticed.

"I never threw another left-handed pitch in my life," I said. "I wasn't that dumb. I eventually realized I'd never be a major league pitcher, righty or lefty. But that one moment was probably the best moment of my life."

Then I looked directly at Mr. Radonski.

"Which is how I came up with the idea for Ambidexterity Week, and why I asked Mr. Radonski to suggest it to the SGC. I just thought it would be cool if other kids could experience what I did. I get that it doesn't really make sense. But I just wanted to see if it could work. And I want to thank Mr. Radonski for agreeing to bring it up for me."

"You're very welcome, Charlie Joe," said Mr. Radonski. Then he looked at Mrs. Sleep. "I told him it was crazy," he added ungratefully.

Mrs. Sleep stood up. "Well, Charles Joseph, that is quite a story. And it appears your intentions were extremely honorable. I'm sorry we can't accommodate an activity such as Ambidexterity Week at this school, but certainly the goal of children learning to use their bodies and minds to the best of their abilities is a noble one, and we must pursue it as vigorously as we can."

I nodded. "Thank you, Mrs. Sleep." Then I picked up the ball. "Even though we're not doing Ambidexterity Week, would it be okay if I threw one last left-handed pitch?"

She still had the glove on her hand. "Absolutely not. This is a school, not a playground."

But then she looked around the room at all the hopeful faces, and for probably the first time in her life, Mrs. Sleep let down her guard. "Just this once, I suppose it would be fine."

She stood up. "Nice and slow," she added. "I'm not exactly Willie Mays."

She held up the glove. I was ready for the big finish. A fastball strike, landing in Mrs. Sleep's glove with the telltale POP! It would be the perfect ending.

But as it turns out, every once in a while the big finish doesn't quite go the way you planned.

I wound up and fired. But I guess my hand was sweaty, and the ball slipped.

Plus, I was throwing lefty. I stink lefty.

The ball headed perfectly straight . . . right at the huge glass window.

Everybody stared.

Time stopped.

CRASH!

Oops.

***

Glass flew everywhere. No one was near the window, luckily, but everyone jumped out of their chairs and screamed. The only one who remained totally calm was Mr. Radonski, who just sat there with a huge smile on his face.

Nareem picked up his gavel and banged it on the table.

"Meeting adjourned," he said.

As we watched the custodial staff clean up the mess—I felt bad and wanted to help, but there was too much broken glass—Katie came up to me.

"How much of that story was true?" she asked. "Or should I say, was any of it true?"

"Some of it was true," I protested. "I did want to be a pitcher. And James Edwards was definitely the best hitter in little league that year." Jerry the custodian gave me my ball back, which was awfully nice of him. I thanked him and turned back to Katie. "But that's not important. A teacher was in trouble, and I was just trying to help him out."

She gave me the old Katie Friedman eye-roll. "You are just incredible."

"In a good way?"

She didn't answer.

***

When my mom came to pick me up and saw the commotion, she asked Mrs. Sleep what happened.

"Your son is a very dynamic storyteller," Mrs. Sleep said, "so I'll let him tell you the story."

"Uh-oh," my mom said.

"At least he's a passionate boy," Mrs. Sleep said. "You must have been quite impressed with his desire to become a left-handed professional baseball player."

My mom just looked at me.

"We should probably go," I said.

And with that, the craziest week of my life was officially over.

Oh, and by the way, the beginning of the next week wasn't exactly a piece of cake, either.

On Monday, I'd been in school about eight seconds when Mrs. Sleep tapped me on the shoulder and said she wanted to see me.

Oh jeez.

We went to her office and Mr. Radonski was waiting there.

"After you left on Friday, Mr. Radonski told me everything," she said.

Oh double jeez.

"Everything what?" I asked.

"That you covered for me," Mr. Radonski said. "I can't have you doing that, kid. I may be hardheaded sometimes, but I'm no cheater. If I mess up, I need to take the hit."

I wasn't sure what to say, so I kept my mouth shut for once.

"Anyway," Mrs. Sleep went on, "what you did was wrong, Charlie Joe. Very wrong. Not to mention destructive."

"That was a total accident!" I protested, mouth no longer shut.

She lowered her head and looked at me over her glasses, which was code for, *I talk, you listen*.

"As I was saying, what you did was wrong. But it was wrong for the right reasons," she said.

Wait—so she thought Camp Rituhbukkee was a bad idea, too?

"You were protecting your teacher," Mrs. Sleep said. "That showed great loyalty and courage. I admire that in a person. Even with the occasional, egregious lack in judgment."

"What does *egregious* mean?" I asked.

"Yeah, what does it mean?" Mr. Radonski asked.

"It means don't do it again," Mrs. Sleep said. Then she looked at Mr. Radonski. "And I don't expect we'll be hearing anymore about Ambidextrous Week, or whatever it was you called it. Isn't that right, Mr. Radonski?"

Mr. Radonski cleared his throat. "That's very right, Mrs. Sleep."

The corners of her lips curled up just enough to be called a smile. It was certainly a smile by Mrs. Sleep standards.

"Have a good day, gentlemen."

On the way out of Mrs. Sleep's office, Mr.

Radonski elbowed me in the stomach and said, "Turns out you're a man after all, Jackson. I owe you one. And your grade is all taken care of."

It felt good being a man.

Especially a man with two A's in his back pocket.

It turned out that getting extra credit was exhausting. Who knew?

I can't believe I'm saying this, but it probably would have been easier to get good grades in the first place.

But then I never would have found out who Byron Chillingsworth was, or met Zoe Alvarez, or figured out how to at least *try* to stand up for your friends, or discovered how sometimes you have to help someone out of a big mess by causing a bigger one, or learned how many dustpans it takes to clean up a shattered, regulation-sized plate-glass window.

Fourteen, for those keeping score at home.

***

But the main thing was, so far my extra-credit plan was working. Two down, one to go. And my academic classes were going really well, too, thanks to the strict studying schedule enforced by my friends. Straight A's were becoming an actual possibility.

What could possibly go wrong?

Charlie Joe's Tip #16

EXTRA CREDIT CAN BE FUN (OCCASIONALLY).

Extra credit is not always work.

Sometimes, you might even enjoy yourself.

For example, watching television. If you sit and watch television with your parents, and you let them pick the show, than you're definitely getting extra credit for being a good son or daughter.

Other fun extra credit activities include:

1. *Eating (when you're at your grand-parents—they love it when you eat).*
2. *Playing video games (when your cousin that nobody knows is over, and you're the one who's forced to entertain him).*
3. *Sleeping (on family road trips, when it's either sleep or annoy your parents).*
4. *Dancing with girls (at the school dance, when no one is dancing and your teacher asks you to break the ice).*
5. *Playing with the dogs (because they've been cooped up all day and your mom says they need some exercise).*

Part Three

EXTRA ABSORBENT

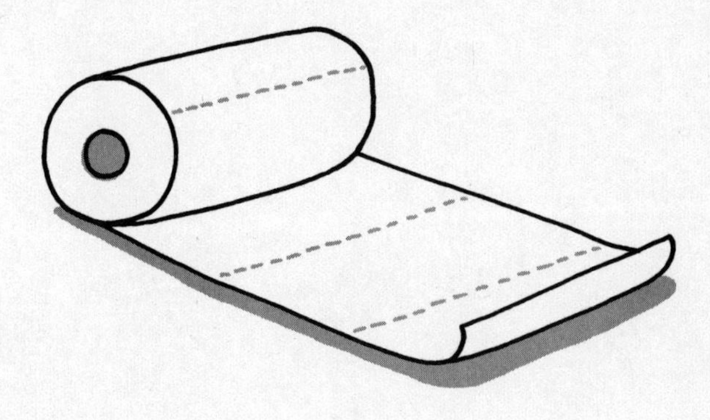

"Does anyone here know who Arthur Scott was?" Mr. Twipple asked.

He was standing on a chair in his classroom, about to announce what the show was going to be. Everyone who was trying out was there. I was half listening and half staring at the giant posters of famous Broadway actors on his walls. (By famous Broadway actors, I mean actors that nobody's ever heard of.)

The drama kids treated this meeting like a really big deal. Isabelle Castle, who was the best singer in the school, couldn't eat a thing at lunch. (She gave me her chocolate milk and Timmy helped himself to her ice cream sandwich.)

There were about thirty people crammed into the room. Evan Franco, my enemy from Drama class, was in the front row sucking up to Mr. Twipple, as usual. I thought he was one hundred percent talent-free, but everybody else considered him the best actor in the school, probably just because he had the same last name as James Franco.

Hannah was there, even though Jake was totally over the idea that she was clingy. He also had decided that he didn't actually want any more free time, and that she didn't have to do the play if she didn't want to. She ignored him, of course.

(Charlie Joe's Girl Tip #1: If you call Hannah Spivero clingy, it will come back to haunt you.)

Nareem was there, too. Turned out he liked acting. "I've been in love with Bollywood films since I was a little child," he told me as we took our seats.

"You mean Hollywood," I said.

"No, I mean Bollywood," he answered.

I scratched my head. Had I just thought it was called Hollywood all these years, but it was really Bollywood?

Nareem saw my confusion. "Bollywood is what they call movies made in India. They're full of colorful acting and wonderful musical sequences."

"Oh," I said.

"I would like to be a Bollywood actor," Nareem said. "Either a Bollywood actor or a physicist."

"Both good choices," I said.

"Why are you here?" asked Nareem. "I did not realize you were keen on the theatrical arts."

"Extra credit."

"Right," Nareem said.

Then Timmy walked in, and I nearly fell off my chair in shock. When I had told him I was trying out, he said "that's hilarious" and couldn't stop laughing. Then I told him Hannah was trying out, and he stopped laughing.

He'd had a thing with Hannah last year, and I'm sure he still liked her, just like the rest of civilization. But trying out for the play just to be near her? That was crazy. I never would have done that. I hope.

Eliza Collins was there, too, in the back row. She fully expected to get the lead role, because all her life she had been told that she looked like a movie star.

"Does anyone know who Arthur Scott is?" Mr. Twipple repeated.

Nobody did.

He turned on his overhead projector and a huge picture came on the screen.

It was a picture of a roll of paper towels.

"Who knows what this is?"

No one said anything. Finally, Eliza raised her hand. "Is this a trick question, Mr. Twipple?"

"No, Eliza, it's not."

Eliza peered at the slide. "Well, then it's a roll of paper towels."

"Exactly right!" Mr. Twipple said. He slammed his hand down on the desk dramatically, which made sense since he was the drama teacher. "It's a roll of paper towels. Paper towels! One of the most forgotten but important inventions in American history. And does anyone know who invented paper towels?"

I was starting to piece the whole thing together, so I raised my hand.

"I'm going to go with Arthur Scott."

Another big desk slam from Mr. Twipple. "Thank you, Charlie Joe! Precisely! Arthur Scott is an American hero, yet nobody knows who he is. But all that is about to change."

Mr. Twipple clicked a button and a new slide came up.

PAPER TIGER: THE LIFE AND LEGEND OF ARTHUR SCOTT

"Ladies and gentlemen, I give you our Spring Theatrical," Mr. Twipple said. Then he clicked to the next slide.

WRITTEN AND DIRECTED BY JEFFREY TWIPPLE

Oh, boy.

The audition turned out to be actually two auditions.

At the first one, we could sing anything we wanted, so I sang "Love Me Do" by The Beatles, the greatest band ever known to man.

But there was another audition, called a Callback.

I guess it's a great honor to be asked to do a Callback because when the list went up outside Mr. Twipple's office, people either jumped for joy or looked like they wanted to cry for a year.

CONGRATULATIONS TO ALL THOSE WHO WERE CALLED BACK, it said on the top of the list. TO THOSE WHO WEREN'T, YOU'RE WELCOME TO JOIN OUR FABULOUS ENSEMBLE!

I didn't know what an ensemble was, but judging by people's reactions, I was pretty sure it wasn't fabulous.

Timmy, Hannah, Eliza, and I were all on the Callback list. So were Isabelle Castle and Evan Franco, of course. But Nareem wasn't. It didn't seem to bother him, though. "I shall be happy just to be a part of the chorus," he said. "Many fine performers got their start in the chorus." I wasn't sure what the difference was between chorus and ensemble, but I didn't care enough to ask.

"Good luck in the Callback," he added.

"Thanks, I'm gonna need it."

I gotta admit, I was kind of irritated that Timmy was called back.

"This is crazy," I said to him. "You can't sing."

It was true, he couldn't sing. But that didn't seem to matter much, because at the audition, he moon-walked like Michael Jackson and jumped like Michael Jordan. He also threw in The Worm, just for fun.

It turned out that Timmy McGibney was the best dancer in the school.

So here we are. This is basically where you came in, way back at the beginning of the book.

Remember? I was standing on the stage of our middle school auditorium, singing a song about paper towels?

"5-6-7-8!" yelled Mr. Twipple, which was obviously some sort of drama code word for "start singing."

We rocked out to the Jeffrey Twipple classic, "Thrills and Spills":

Wiping up messes!
Brushing off dresses!
There's nothing paper towels can't do . . .
Cleaning up crumbs!
No matter what accident comes!
There's nothing paper towels can't do . . .

I looked at Timmy, who was on the other side of the stage. He looked just as miserable as me. Which made me feel a little better.

Hannah, of course, turned out to be a really good singer, dancer, and actor. (Duh. She's good at everything, remember?) So good, in fact, that Isabelle Castle started to get nervous. So she sang louder. Which made Hannah sing even louder. Soon everyone was covering their ears.

Game on.

Meanwhile, Eliza Collins quickly realized that both girls were way better than her, so she decided not to care and started goofing around with Evan Franco. He actually did care, but he was so freaked out by how pretty Eliza was that he laughed at all her bad jokes.

Bad move.

Mr. Twipple stopped the music. "Eliza and Evan, this isn't a comedy club, it is a theater. If you'd rather make jokes, please leave."

Evan looked like he was about to cry. It was fantastic.

"The last section again, please," Mr. Twipple barked. "5-6-7-8!"

It gives me a thrill
Every time I stop and sop up a spill
There's nothing, no nothing, that paper towels can't
Do-oooh-oooh-oooh!

***

We did the song about three more times, and learned a dance step that involved a lot of jumping and wiping. Finally, Mr. Twipple told us to stop. We stood on the stage, panting, while he made notes on a pad.

"Very nice job everyone. The cast list will be posted on Monday."

As I was getting ready to leave, Hannah came over to me.

"Isn't this fun, Charlie Joe?"

I looked at her. "It's not as bad as I thought it was going to be, I guess."

Then, out of nowhere, she gave me a big hug. "How's Zoe? I'm really looking forward to going to the movies with you guys tomorrow night. She seems great. I'm glad you found her. I'm really glad you guys are together."

"Who said I found her? And I told you the other day, we're not together."

But she didn't answer. Instead, she just hugged me again and left.

As I watched her go, I realized I'd figured out one thing about girls.

They're impossible to figure out.

That night, I went to the town library with Nareem and Katie to study for an English test.

That's right, you heard me. The town library. To study for a test.

I know. I was as shocked as you are.

I looked around the library. "Wow, it's packed," I said, using my outside voice.

"Shush!" Katie whispered.

"Sorry. Out of practice."

But it was kind of shocking to see how many people were at the library.

It was a festival of reading and studying. Hopefully some people were playing video games on computers, but I couldn't be sure.

"Don't these people have anything better to do?" I asked.

"They come here because they would like to get good grades without having to rely on extra credit and help from friends," said Nareem.

"What's your point?" I asked.

"Life doesn't have to be as difficult as you make it, is his point," Katie said.

"Meaning what?"

"Meaning, you hate to read, but you spend more time figuring out how to avoid it than you would reading in the first place. And you love to annoy teachers, so you spend all this time getting extra credit, instead of just not annoying them in the first place."

"It's a bit of a pattern, I'm afraid," Nareem added.

They looked at each other, smiling and nodding, and suddenly it hit me.

"Do you two like, like each other or something?"

Katie giggled but didn't say anything.

"We respect each other a great deal," Nareem said. "Let's leave it at that, shall we?"

"Fine. You leave me alone about my study habits, and I'll leave you guys alone about your little romance."

We found an empty table and sat down.

Nareem opened up his backpack. "Shall we get to work? Let's start with vocabulary." He flipped open a notebook. "What does *stubborn* mean?"

"It means Charlie Joe," Katie said, before I could say anything.

The next night was movie night. And when two middle school boys go to the movies with two middle school girls, the arrangements are kind of weird. Meaning, everybody gets driven separately, and they all meet up at the theater. I don't know why, but that's just the way it is.

My mom always drove me. We had an arrangement. In exchange for giving me rides, she was allowed to bombard me with questions.

"What movie are you guys seeing?" she asked.

"Not sure."

"So you like Zoe? Meaning, *like* like?"

"I don't know, Mom."

"Sure you do."

I sighed. The thing about parents is that they absolutely, positively never give up trying to get personal information out of their kids. No matter how hopeless it is.

"And what about Hannah?" she added. "You're over her at last? Finally moving on? After all these years? Could it be?"

There was only one answer to that.

I turned up the radio.

When I went inside the theater, Jake, Hannah, and Zoe were already there. They'd gotten candy and popcorn, and sodas the size of a small country.

Zoe saw me first and came running up to me.

"You're late!"

"I'm only late when my mom can't find her glasses. Which is always."

We hugged, and then immediately felt shy about it.

Jake and Hannah walked over.

"Dude," Jake said, which is something he only calls me in front of Hannah. Then he gave me the bro handshake, which was half handshake, half hug.

Hannah gave me a big hug—unnecessarily big, I thought.

"Mr. Actor!" She kept on hugging me—unnecessarily long, I thought.

Zoe and Jake looked at her.

"You should have seen Charlie Joe in the audition," Hannah gushed, staring at me. "He was totally amazing. He's a born performer, I swear." If I didn't know better I would have sworn she was totally flirting with me, right in front of Jake and Zoe.

"That's great," Zoe said uncomfortably.

Hannah nodded. "Yeah, I think we're totally going to have an awesome time together in this show, right, Charlie Joe?"

I was starting to feel weird. "I guess."

Jake tried to hold Hannah's hand. But Hannah wouldn't take it. Instead, she just kept smiling at me.

And that's when it hit me. That's when I finally realized what Hannah was up to.

She was mad at Jake for calling her clingy. And she was mad at me for liking someone who wasn't her.

So she decided to do the school play to get back at both of us.

I suddenly got madder than I've ever been in my entire life. Because Hannah, who had always been the all-time perfect girl, turned out to be just like anyone else.

Human.

"You know what?" I said. "I don't think I'm going to do the play. The whole thing is dumb."

Hannah looked shocked. "That's crazy," she said. "You're probably going to get a really good part. And we can totally hang out." Then she smiled at me again.

But I didn't smile back.

"Didn't Jake already say sorry for calling you clingy?" I asked, raising my voice a little. "You don't have to put on this big show of wanting to be my best friend just to get back at him, you know."

Zoe and Jake looked at each other, not sure what to do.

Hannah laughed nervously. "What are you talking about?"

"And I know why you're suddenly paying lots of attention to me," I said, plowing ahead. "Because I might actually like another girl. Well, guess what? Your game's not working. Because I like Zoe, and I might like her even more than I ever liked you!"

"Charlie Joe, stop it," Zoe said.

"Why?" I said to her. "I'm not being a wimp for once! What, you're the only one who can stand up for yourself? You should be proud of me instead of trying to stop me."

Zoe turned bright red and looked at her shoes. I immediately felt like a complete jerk, but I was too stubborn and too mad to admit it.

Jake and Hannah stared at me in shock.

"You're totally not being fair," Hannah whispered. "I just thought it would be fun, that's all."

I couldn't look at her, because I didn't want to give in. "It is fair, and you know it."

She started to cry. "Why did you want to go to the movies with Jake and Zoe and me? So Jake could spend more time with his friends? I doubt it. You just wanted to announce to the world you finally liked someone else, and then show her off right in front of me."

"That's not true," I said, but I think all of us knew that it was.

"It IS true!" Hannah yelled. "And guess what? It worked. Just because you've always thought I'm some kind of perfect person doesn't mean I am a perfect person! I have feelings too and you're making me feel really bad!" Then she ran out of the movie theater without another word.

The rest of us stood there silently for what seemed like a week. Finally, Jake turned to me.

"You're doing the play," he said.

"What?"

"You're doing it," he said. "You need the extra credit."

I hadn't even thought about what quitting the play would do to my grade. A chill ran down my spine thinking about Camp Rituhbukkee.

"I'll figure something out," I said. "Maybe I'll help out backstage or something."

"No," Jake insisted. "You're doing the play. Hannah said you're a really good actor. And you need to get an A. Even though you can be a real jerk sometimes—like now, for instance—everyone wants you around this summer. So we'll figure all this out, everything will get back to normal. Just don't quit the play." He tried to smile. "And don't blow it with Zoe, she seems incredible."

And then he ran out after his girlfriend.

Watching him go, I realized that Jake was one of the most annoying people I knew.

While I was busy failing at being a good person, Jake was constantly reminding me what it meant to be a really, really great person.

Who can compete with that?

***

After they left, I turned to Zoe. "I'm going to get some Milk Duds. Do you want some?"

She looked like she was about to cry, too. "I think we should probably just go."

"You sure?"

She nodded.

As we waited for our parents, we didn't talk much. But when her mom came, she turned to me.

"I'm not sure we should hang out anymore."

I looked at her in shock. "What? What did I do?

"You say you want to be able to stand up for yourself, that's fine. But that doesn't give you the right to hurt other people."

I didn't know what to say. I tried to say "I'm sorry," but

the words wouldn't come out. She started walking to her car, then turned back to me.

"And besides, if you like Hannah Spivero, you should have just told me," she said, and left.

***

My mom came five minutes later.

"What was that about? Where are the other kids? Is everything okay? What happened?"

"The projector broke," I said.

CAST LIST

Fred Wimple...............Evan Franco
Betty Wimple.............Isabelle Castle
Little Jack Scott ....Timmy McGibney
Mary Scott.................Hannah Spivero
Arthur Scott ....Charlie Joe Jackson

Assorted Townspeople, Factory Workers and Ensemble: Lisbeth Akers, Chrissy Birnbaum, Eliza Collins, George Delaney, Barbara Fitzer, Richard Hawthorne, Tessa Jenkins, Darryle Kincaid, Jamie Poole, Nareem Ramdal, Jennifer Sarnoff, Ellen Wickerstaff, Julianna Yaeger.

59

I stared at the sheet of paper, my heart racing.

Arthur Scott?

The lead role? I got the lead role and Evan Franco didn't?!?!

I couldn't believe it. Actually, I didn't believe it, until everyone started pounding me on the back, screaming "Way to go!" and "Charlie Joe got the lead!" and "No way!"

We were crowded around Mr. Twipple's bulletin board. Kids were screaming and yelling. One or two were crying, I think. People were making so much noise that other people who had never thought about the school play in their lives, like Pete Milano and his pimply friend Eric, came wandering over.

"What's going on?" Pete demanded.

"The cast list just went up," someone said.

"Oooh, the cast list!" Eric said, jumping around like an idiot. "I'm so excited! The cast list!"

Pete examined the list. Then he looked at me. "Dude, you're on there! You tried out for the play?"

I nodded.

"He got the lead," said Jennifer Sarnoff, who was really short, wore glasses, and wasn't afraid of anyone. "So you better congratulate him. NOW."

"Congratulations," Pete mumbled. (He was probably having flashbacks of Zoe, and didn't want to be humiliated by another girl.)

"Dude, let's get out of here before we catch actor-itis," Eric said, and they ran down the hall, cracking up.

"Don't come back," Jennifer yelled after them. Then she turned to me. "Are those jerks friends of yours?"

"Not really," I said, nervously. I'd never been scared of a tiny girl nerd before. It was a weird feeling.

"I hope not," she said. "And congratulations. You're going to be great." She gave me a big hug.

Evan Franco came up to me. "Congratulations," he said.

"Congratulations to you, too," I answered. I guess if he was trying to be nice about it, so would I.

But it turned out he didn't want to be that nice. "You better be good," he said, and he walked away. "Hannah better be good, too."

Hannah. I hadn't talked to her since our fight at the

movie theater, and now it turned out we were going to be playing a married couple.

Life's funny that way.

I saw Timmy down the hall, accepting congratulations from three girls in the ensemble. I'd never seen him so happy in his life, and I realized he must be feeling the same way I was. I'd never even considered doing the school play before, and now I realized I was pretty excited.

It was kind of embarrassing and kind of awesome all at the same time.

But Hannah was nowhere to be found. I finally got Timmy away from his fan club and asked him if he had seen Hannah.

"Yeah, I heard she was in the bathroom."

"Really? That's a weird place to be celebrating."

He shook his head. "Dude, she's not celebrating. She's with Isabelle."

I still didn't get it. "So they're celebrating together? In the bathroom?"

"No, man. They're not celebrating. Isabelle is in there crying her eyes out because she didn't get the lead girl. Hannah's trying to make her feel better."

Wow. This school play stuff was even more competitive than sports.

Extra credit wasn't for wimps.

I had two interesting text exchanges that night.

The first one was from Zoe:

CONGRATULATIONS

Thanks

THE LEAD ROLE THAT'S GREAT

I know, it's crazy.

AND HANNAH GOT THE OTHER LEAD PART?

Yeah.

THAT'S COOL

You're not mad?

NO I'M NOT MAD

Can we maybe hang out again sometime?

WE'LL SEE

Ok cool

TTYL

***

The second was from Jake:

DUDE CONGRATS THAT'S AWESOME.

I know, it's crazy.

SO HANNAH'S PLAYING YOUR WIFE?

I guess so.

WOW.

I know right?

YEAH. WEIRD.

Dude you're the one who told me I had to do the play.

I CAN'T BELIEVE I EVER CALLED HER CLINGY. WHAT A MORON I AM.

You're telling me!!

WATCH IT.

Sorry.

GTG

K later.

"Charlie Joe, I'd like to speak with you for a quick moment," Mr. Twipple said to me just before the first rehearsal.

I figured he was going to tell me that he'd made a terrible mistake. I knew it. I knew I shouldn't have gotten all excited! School plays are stupid and dorky and—

"Congratulations on getting the part of Arthur Scott," he said.

Okay, so scratch that whole school-plays-are-dorky thing.

"It's a big responsibility," he added. "Do you think you can handle it?"

I nodded.

"Good." He pointed down at his script. "I cast you because you have the same qualities as Arthur Scott. He didn't play by the rules. He wasn't afraid of anyone. He pushed boundaries. And he changed the world. I want to see those qualities in your performance."

"Sounds good."

He put his hands on my shoulders. "However. As an actor in my cast, you *do* have to play by the rules, and you have to stay *within* the boundaries. I demand that as a director. Got it?"

So he wanted me to be rebellious, but do exactly what he said.

"Got it."

He handed me my script. "Let's get to work."

***

It turned out that pretty much the only thing Mr. Twipple knew about Arthur Scott was that he invented paper towels.

"I've taken a few liberties with Mr. Scott's life to make it more dramatically appealing to the audience," is how he put it.

Meaning, he made a lot of stuff up.

The plot of *Paper Tiger: The Life and Legend of Arthur Scott* sounded a lot like an action-adventure movie. Arthur Scott, his wife, Mary, and their ten-year-old son, Little Jack, arrive from Scotland (get it?) on a tiny boat that somehow survives pirates, sharks, and a horrible storm. After they land in America, Arthur builds his paper company from scratch, only to be threatened by jealous rival Fred Wimple and his wife, Betty. Arthur and Fred have a huge sword fight, because of a disagreement over who invented tissues, and Arthur gets wounded. He decides to move back to Scotland to go into his family's celery-farming business. But then Little Jack gets tuberculosis, Mary and Betty realize that life is precious and they become friends, and Arthur and Fred team up to fight off a new rival, William (Big Will) Brawny. With Fred's help, Arthur invents paper towels! Little Jack recovers, and they all live happily ever after.

When I showed the script to my dad, he laughed and said, "What is this, Indiana Jones and the Temple of Toilet Paper?"

But my mom loved it. "I think it's going to be wonderful, and you're going to be wonderful in it," she said. Then she gave me one of those big Mom hugs that feel so good, even though part of you thinks you're too old for a hug like that.

"My son the star," she whispered in my ear.

"Your son the kid who is going to spend his summer sleeping until noon, playing video games with my friends, and eating French fries at the beach," I whispered back, but I wasn't sure she heard me.

Charlie Joe's Tip #17

NEVER DO EXTRA CREDIT ON WEEKENDS.

Some things are sacred.

Chocolate. The Beatles. Sleep. Funny movies. The first time you dive into a pool at the beginning of summer.

And weekends.

They're called weekends for a reason. The week has ended. That means, all the things that people associate with the week have ended. Like school, and homework, and waking up early, and limited video game use.

Extra-credit projects definitely fall into the "during the week" category. So if someone ever suggests doing an extra-credit project that involves the weekend—like a project for a science fair, for example, or taking a trip to the United Nations—you politely decline.

Weekends are your own. Never forget that.

What Jake said at the movie theater turned out to be right: over the next two weeks, everything pretty much got back to normal. Hannah and Jake seemed happy again, which was great, kind of. I kept getting good grades on tests, which, now that I think about it, wasn't really normal at all.

The only thing that was still weird was Zoe. We were friendly and stuff, but it wasn't the same as before.

And the less like before it was, the more like before I wanted it to be.

Because here's the thing: I'll just come out and say it. I really liked Zoe. But it's really complicated to like one girl, and still kind of be hung up on another. Because no matter what, Hannah was still Hannah, and there was nothing I could do about that.

Besides, we had to pretend to be married every day after school.

Rehearsals were going pretty well. I had a bunch of lines to memorize, which was scary at first, but turned out to be not as hard as I thought. We spent a ton of time on the sword-fighting scene, which was actually really fun even though the swords were made out of this rubbery plastic stuff. And we worked a lot on the finale, which was a big slow song called "Lessons Worth Absorbing."

Then, during the last week of rehearsal, Mr. Twipple called Hannah and me into his office.

"I've decided the two of you should kiss at the end of the last scene. Do you think you can handle that?"

Hannah and I looked at each other.

"Sounds okay, I guess," I said, trying to remain cool even though it was the one thing I'd thought about for like six years.

Hannah didn't say anything. She was still acting a little mad at me, even though I had stopped being mad at her like forever ago. Girls hold grudges longer than boys—it's a fact of life.

"Hannah, what do you say?" Mr. Twipple asked again.

She looked right at me. "Do we have to rehearse it?"

"No," answered Mr. Twipple. "We'll wait until the actual performance. I don't need your parents calling me up and saying I'm promoting public displays of affection."

"Okay," Hannah said, finally.

"I really think we should practice it to make sure we get it right," I said. Hannah couldn't help giggling a little. Mr. Twipple shook his head.

"Somehow I think you'll be able to figure it out."

63

The next day, Evan Franco and Eliza Collins came up to me in the lunch line. They'd been hanging out a lot ever since the audition. Evan was in heaven.

"Charlie Joe!" said Evan. "Mr. Leading Man." He was definitely still bitter about me getting the best part, since he was the one who took singing lessons.

"Charlie Joe, you're so good in the part," gushed Eliza, much to Evan's irritation.

"Thanks."

Evan ordered his meatball hero, then turned back to me. "Hey, I've been meaning to ask you—does Zoe know that you get to kiss Hannah in the show?"

"Oh yeah, does she?" Eliza chimed in.

"Huh?"

"Did you tell her?" they both said at the same time.

As it turned out, I hadn't been able to find the right time to tell her. Probably because the right time didn't exist.

I shook my head.

Evan took a long slurp of orange juice. "A love triangle. Must be pretty distracting."

"It's not a love triangle," I said. "It's just a part in a play."

Eliza laughed. "Oh Charlie Joe, we're totally just kidding! Keep up the great work."

"Yeah, totally keep it up," Evan added. "Just don't lose focus. And when you're about to kiss her during the show, just make sure you don't look into the audience. That would be the worst thing you could do."

They walked away, Eliza giggling, and Evan making that annoying sound you make with your straw when you keep sucking after the juice is gone.

I stood there for a second. That was a weird little conversation. I needed to clear my head. So I did what any confused person would have done.

I ate three chocolate puddings instead of two.

On the last day of rehearsal, Hannah started coughing.

"You're not getting sick, are you?" I asked. I was concerned about her health. I was also concerned about missing the opportunity to kiss her the next night.

We were practicing the first scene, where Arthur, Mary, and Little Jack take the boat to America and get attacked by pirates. Nareem was playing one of the pirates and he had me in a pirate death grip. Then Timmy, who was playing Little Jack, came over and cracked Pirate Nareem over the head with a fake oar.

"Ow!" Nareem screamed, very convincingly.

"Are you okay?" asked Hannah.

"STOP!" yelled Mr. Twipple. He stared at Hannah. "Why are you asking him if he's okay? He's a pirate and he just attacked your ship!"

Hannah shrugged. "It seemed like he was really hurt."

"It's called acting," Mr. Twipple hissed.

"You're a good actor," Hannah said to Nareem, who blushed.

She coughed again. Maybe she *was* getting sick. Everyone stared at her.

"Well, this is great timing. What's going on with you?" said Mr. Twipple.

"I'll be fine," she said, but then coughed again.

Mr. Twipple cleared his throat. "Everyone, may I have your attention. A physical reaction, such as Ms. Spivero is experiencing, can often be a sign of nerves—the beginnings of what is called stage fright. Stage fright occurs when actors become nervous about performing in public. A little nervousness is natural, even healthy, but stage fright can be very, very dangerous. As actors, you must all take great care never to give in to stage fright."

Evan Franco came over to me. "Is she okay?" he whispered. "Maybe Zoe can play her part instead."

"Buzz off," I said.

The whole cast surrounded Hannah, wanting to know if she was okay. They were totally treating her like she was the most important person on earth.

Join the club, people.

Then Eliza, who was having a hard time not being the center of attention for once, started coughing, too.

But no one cared.

Charlie Joe's Tip #18

WHEN IT COMES RIGHT DOWN TO IT, EXTRA CREDIT ISN'T OPTIONAL.

Wikipedia is amazing. But it's not always 100 percent accurate. For example, here's how they define *extra credit*:

Extra credit is an academic concept, particularly used in American schools. Students are offered the opportunity to undertake optional work, additional to their compulsory schoolwork, in order to gain additional credit that would boost their grades.

Perfectly reasonable explanation. But incorrect. Extra credit isn't optional. It might sound optional, but it's not.

Here's why people go for extra credit:

1. *They don't want to be grounded.*
2. *They don't want to lose video game privileges.*
3. *They don't want to lose their cell phone.*

4. *They don't want to go without dessert for a month.*
5. *They don't want to go to reading camp.*

Do you see anything optional there? I don't.

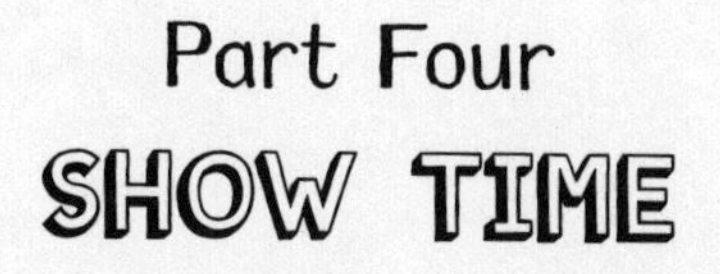

Part Four
SHOW TIME

The morning of our performance—which was technically called Opening Night, even though there was only one night—my mom made my favorite breakfast: French toast, scrambled eggs and a chocolate croissant.

"Such a big star," she said.

I devoured it, and then burped loudly.

"But still my son."

I started getting butterflies around lunchtime.

I think Mr. Twipple's speech about stage fright was starting to get to me. My mouth was totally dry. I was dying of thirst but I wasn't hungry. I was staring at my chocolate pudding, unable to eat a bite.

When you can't eat pudding, you know it's serious.

Everyone was talking about the play. EVERYONE. I had no idea it was such a big thing, because I personally had always ignored everything about it, but pretty much the whole school was excited to go see it. I was shocked.

Katie was sitting next to me at lunch, and as usual, she was reading me like a book. (A short book, hopefully.)

"You'll be fine. Seriously. You're going to kill."

"Is kill good?"

She patted my back. "Yes, dear."

Jake and Hannah were hanging out by themselves at the next table over (he was totally over the "clingy" thing, obviously). Her cough was gone, and she didn't look nervous at all. Life is so unfair.

Then I saw Zoe. She was walking towards me, with one of those smiles from before things got a little weird at the movie theater.

"Can I talk to you for a minute?"

"Sure."

We went to an empty table. I could tell everyone was watching us. But you know what? So what.

"Hi," she said.

"Hi."

She reached into her backpack and got out two chocolate milks.

"I thought you might be thirsty," she said, and handed me one.

I think it might have been the nicest present anyone ever gave me.

"Thanks," I said, draining it in one gulp.

She giggled. "You're nervous."

"I guess."

Then she took my hand. "Don't be. You'll be great. I can't wait to see it."

Then she reached into her backpack again, and this time she pulled out a poster she made. It was made out of paper towels, and it said. GOOD LUCK ARTHUR SCOTT! LOVE, YOUR BIGGEST FAN, ZOE.

I stared at it. "That is awesome." Then I stared at the floor. "Zoe, I'm really sorry I yelled at you at the movie theater. I was just trying to stand up for myself, the way you always do, and I guess I got all mixed up. That was really stupid."

I looked up at her. She was smiling. "That's okay," she

said. "I was totally stupid, too. It's none of my business if you like Hannah. I don't have any right to be mad about that, and I'm sorry."

"But I—" I started to say I don't like Hannah, but I couldn't quite go through with it. Instead I simply said, "I like *you*."

"I like you, too."

She hugged me. I hugged her. And then I noticed Hannah staring at us.

Girls are so freakin' complicated.

Suddenly Pete Milano came running up. "Dudes, guess what I just heard?" he yelled.

He waited until he had everyone's full attention.

"There's gonna be some kissin' and huggin' in the show tonight! That's right! Charlie Joe and Hannah have like a MASSIVE MAKE-OUT SESSION at the end of the play!" He ran over to Jake and punched him in the arm. "Dude, your girlfriend is like totally gonna be mackin' with another man tonight. RIGHT IN FRONT OF THE WHOLE TOWN!"

Everybody was staring at Hannah and me.

"No way," Katie said, quietly. "That's intense."

I got up to face Pete. "Who told you that? Who told you?"

"A little birdie," he said, but I saw his eyes glance off to the side. I followed his eyes and saw Evan and Eliza, giggling in a corner. Well, she was giggling. He was shrugging his shoulders and saying, "I'm sorry," which of course he didn't mean.

Zoe looked up at me. "Is that true?"

Before I could answer, Hannah did. "It doesn't mean anything, I swear," she said, walking over to Zoe. "And Jake's not worried about it, so you don't have to be either."

Everyone looked at Jake. He looked like he was trying his best to not be worried about it, but he wasn't quite pulling it off.

Zoe looked at me. Her smile was gone. Then she got up and walked away.

I was completely confused. I'd dreamt about kissing Hannah since I basically found out what kissing was.

How can something be a dream come true and a nightmare all at the same time?

I got to school an hour before the show, but the parking lot was already full. The whole town was there. The whole school was there. Mr. Radonski was there, with his wife, who was gorgeous (go figure). Ms. Ferrell was there. Mrs. Sleep was there. Mrs. Massey was there.

Pete Milano was there with a couple of his soccer buddies.

Zoe was there with her parents. In the row in front of her were Jake and his parents. And five seats over from them were my sister Megan and my parents.

From backstage, I looked out at the packed auditorium and suddenly felt a little sick to my stomach.

Evan Franco came up to me. "Nervous?"

"Stay away from me."

"Dude, what's the big deal? People were going to find out about the big kiss sooner or later. Would you rather have them discover it when you're actually making out with Hannah right in front of them? Eliza and I totally did you a favor."

"Have a good show," I said, and walked away.

The lights went down. The orchestra—well, the piano player, violin player, and drummer, which Mr. Twipple liked to call "the orchestra"—started playing.

The ensemble gathered in this giant cardboard box, which was supposed to represent the boat to America.

They started singing the first song, "America Is Calling":

America is calling
And I hear her now
America is calling
And I will answer somehow . . .

At that point, Hannah and Timmy came out, as Mary and Little Jack Scott.

Hannah sang:

America is going to be our new home, where our dreams will shine through!

Then Timmy sang:

America is where I will learn to be brave and strong and true!

That's when Arthur Scott makes his big entrance. I was petrified, but somehow I managed to run onto the stage. I could feel a wave of energy race through the auditorium as I went to my mark (that's what you call the place I'm supposed to stand), took Hannah's and Timmy's hands, and started singing:

America is calling
Oh yes, she is calling
America is calling to me and to you!

The whole cast joined in:

America is calling to me and to you!
To me and to you!

All of a sudden, I wasn't nervous anymore.

Then the pirates attacked, and we were off and running.

Charlie Joe's Tip #19

WHEN YOUR EXTRA CREDIT PROJECT GOES WRONG, RUN THE OTHER WAY.

Just kidding. My actual advice is, close your eyes and pray.

The first act went by in a blur. It ends with the big swordfight, while Hannah and Isabelle sing a song called "Why Do Men Act Like Boys?" When I get wounded, Timmy enters and does a big healing dance while Hannah bandages me up. Then the whole cast comes out and sings "Tissues," a slow song that somehow combines a cry for peace with a description of certain kinds of paper products.

It's not quite as ridiculous as it sounds. Almost, but not quite.

***

At intermission, we all drank water and jabbered at each other about how fantastic it was going.

"We rock! This is intense! They totally love it! You're doing totally awesome!"

Stuff like that.

Mr. Twipple gathered us in a circle.

"I'm so proud of each and every one of you. It's really going terrifically well. Let's have a great second act."

It was time for Act II.

Otherwise known as, The Act Where I Kiss Hannah.

Eliza squeezed my arm. "Have fun," she said, with a wink, as the lights went down.

Charlie Joe's Tip #20

EXTRA CREDIT DOESN'T MAKE YOU SMARTER.

Extra credit is great because it can help you get your grades up.

But just because your grades are higher doesn't mean you're suddenly a smarter person.

And it doesn't mean you're suddenly going to make all the right decisions.

Because unfortunately, life has a habit of making its own plans.

Life is funny that way.

The cast was even more on fire during the second act. Timmy danced his butt off, Isabelle was amazing, Evan did a great job (much as I hate to admit it), and the part where we actually invent the paper towel—during a song called "Changing the World, One Spill at a Time"—was totally intense.

Then suddenly, it was just me and Hannah out on the stage, singing the big finale.

We sang:

Lessons worth absorbing
Are the most important lessons of all
Love and family
And learning how to stand tall
Lessons worth absorbing
Are a gift from up above
And the most absorbing lesson of all
Is learning how to love.

That's when we kiss.

On the lips.

It was the moment we'd all been waiting for.

Well, the moment I'd been waiting for, anyway.

Hannah looked at me. I looked at her. She waited. And then, for some reason, I started thinking about what Evan Franco had told me: *Whatever you do, don't look into the audience.*

So of course, I looked into the audience.

The first person I saw was Jake Katz, watching Hannah with complete and utter devotion.

Suddenly I realized how hilarious it was that he had ever called her clingy. Who was he kidding? He was as crazy about her as ever. And he looked nervous, which made me feel guilty.

Then I saw Zoe. She was at the edge of her seat. And she was watching *me* with complete and utter confusion. And she looked kind of scared, which also made me feel guilty.

I quickly scanned the entire audience. They were on the edge of their seats.

I turned back to Hannah. I leaned into her. She leaned into me. This was it . . .

And I *froze*.

I couldn't do it.

I couldn't kiss her. It just didn't feel right.

I stood there for what felt like a week, looked one last time at the audience, looked back at Hannah, mumbled "I'm sorry," and I ran off the stage.

I was pretty sure I heard Evan Franco giggle as I ran by.

Mr. Twipple was waiting for me offstage.

"Charlie Joe! What on earth are you doing?"

"I can't kiss Hannah. It's a long story."

He started pacing. "What? What? Are you kidding? You've been looking forward to kissing her for three weeks. And besides, you're an actor! You've got to get out there and finish the show! FINISH THE SHOW!"

"I'm not an actor, actually. You shouldn't have cast me. I just wanted extra credit to get an A and not have to go to summer reading camp. That's what this was all about. Sorry."

Mr. Twipple looked about as disappointed as I've ever seen a person look. "People told me I should have cast Evan, but I didn't listen to them. I really thought you could do this, Charlie Joe. You had me totally fooled. So I guess you are a good actor, huh? Just not when it counts."

I looked out at the stage. The cast was waiting. The audience was murmuring. I looked out into the audience and saw Ms. Ferrell.

She smiled at me, and I felt a little better.

Then I saw my parents. They were pointing at the stage, giving me the thumbs up.

And then I saw Zoe.

And I saw her lips move.

"It's okay," they said. "You can do it. You can."

But I still couldn't move. Then I felt a smack on my back. It was Timmy.

"Are you kidding dude? Get back out there! You're doing fantastic, and we got a show to finish! And you get to kiss Hannah! Come on!" And he smacked me on the back again, harder.

I guess that woke me up.

I looked at Timmy, my oldest friend, my most annoying friend, and my best friend, and realized he was right. So was Ms. Ferrell. So was Mr. Twipple. So was my family. And so was Zoe.

We had a show to finish. And I had a girl to kiss.

When I got back out to the center of the stage, Hannah was waiting for me like nothing had happened.

"Are you ready?" she asked.

"Yes," I answered.

I leaned in to kiss her but I hesitated again, for just a second. But this time Hannah wasn't taking any chances. She put her hands on my head, turned me toward her, and kissed me full on the lips, for like five seconds.

It was kind of the greatest moment of my life.

The crowd went wild. Even Jake and Zoe.

Hannah finally released me.

"Not so terrible, was it?" she said.

***

The rest of the cast joined us on stage to sing the last verse:

Lessons worth absorbing
Are what makes the world go round
Every thing we do and touch

Every sight and every sound
Lessons worth absorbing
Taught to every boy and girl
Will be the only way
We can clean up this world.

Timmy did one last dance, which ends with him wiping a giant paper towel over a map of the world, and the show was over.

For a second, the whole place was silent. The cast didn't move.

Then the audience erupted. A huge standing ovation! THEY LOVED IT!

We bowed: first the ensemble, then Timmy, then Evan and Isabelle. Finally, Hannah and I walked down the center of the stage to take our bow. The place went nuts.

It was the new greatest moment of my life.

***

During the curtain call at the end of the show, when we all take our bows, Jake came running down the aisle and gave Hannah a bouquet of flowers.

She thanked him by kissing him on the lips.

I could tell she wasn't acting.

In the lobby after the show, the whole cast got mobbed. It was kind of like The Beatles when they got off the plane in America for the first time. It was crazy.

And you know what? Not one person mentioned the whole running-off-the-stage thing. Not even Pete Milano!

It made me realize how people can be so totally nice sometimes.

Katie was the first to reach me. She just kept saying, "You were amazing, that was amazing," over and over. Then she went off to find Nareem.

Mrs. Massey hugged me and said, "Would you be interested in posing for me as Arthur Scott?"

"I'll think about it," I said.

"I'm just kidding," she said, and hugged me again.

Mr. Radonski came up with his wife. He shook my hand.

"Quite a show, kid," he said.

"Thanks, Mr. Radonski."

"Really wonderful," his wife added. I wanted to ask why someone as pretty as her was married to Mr. Radonski, but it didn't seem like the right time.

"See you in SGC on Wednesday," he said, smacking my back. "I've got some big new ideas." Then he smacked me on the back again and walked away.

Ms. Ferrell was my next admirer. "Quite the performer."

"Thanks."

"I hope you have a wonderful summer," she said, winking.

I winked back. "I hope so, too."

Pete ran up and gave me a high five that nearly took my hand off. "Dude! Unreal, dude! Totally unreal!"

I saw my parents and Megan, trying to work their way through the crowd. They waved to me, and I waved back. Finally they reached me. Megan gave me flowers. "That was awesome! You're like a real actor!"

My mom couldn't talk, because she was crying a little. She just hugged me for a while.

"Really something," my dad said, shaking his head. "Really something." And then he hugged me, too, but for not as long as my mom.

The last person to reach me was Zoe.

She didn't say anything. She just kissed me on the left cheek. Her go-to cheek for kisses.

"I'm so glad you came," I said. "You're not mad?"

She punched me on the arm.

"How can I be mad at a guy for kissing his wife?"

After the show, we had a cast party in the cafeteria, with all my favorite treats: ice cream, chocolate chip cookies, caramel apples, and cream soda (I made sure my mom was on the refreshments committee).

Mr. Twipple shushed the room by raising his hand, the same way he did at rehearsal, and gave a short speech.

"When I wrote this play, I could never have dreamed that it could be done with such superb artistry and professionalism. Thank you, each and every one of you, for everything you did to bring it to life so beautifully."

"WE LOVE YOU, MR. TWIPPLE!" screamed the girls, as he went out into the hallway to accept congratulations from the parents.

Then Evan Franco climbed up onto a chair.

"I'd like to make a toast as well."

Uh oh. I didn't like the sound of that.

"Here's to the cast and crew of *Paper Tiger,*" Evan began, "for putting on such a great show."

Everybody cheered.

"To Timmy, for being such a great dancer. To Isabelle, for being such a great wife. And to Eliza, for being my off-stage wife, someday, if I'm lucky."

Everybody laughed and cheered some more.

"And to Hannah, for being such a great kisser, right Charlie Joe?"

Loudest cheers of all.

"And lastly," Evan said, looking straight at me, "to the man who got the leading part, and then got the worst case of stage fright I've ever seen."

The cheering stopped. Everyone looked at me.

My heart started to pound.

He raised his glass. "He taught us all that the show must go on . . . eventually! Even if everybody has to wait five minutes so he can get up the courage to actually kiss a girl. So here's to Charlie Joe!"

Evan took a drink of his soda. "Oh, and if you're totally freaking out when you're about to kiss Zoe, just give me a call. I'll be happy to help out."

Everyone started whispering, waiting to see how I would react.

Evan stood there with this sickening smirk on his face, waiting for people to tell him how funny he was. Nobody did. Not even Eliza, who just looked embarrassed.

I wasn't sure what to do. The same old doubts crept up inside me. How many times was I going to let someone make a fool out of me?

I looked around, unable to move. Then all of a sudden I saw Zoe, standing at the door, watching me, waiting to see what I would do. She nodded. I nodded. And suddenly, I knew what I was going to do.

I pointed at the caramel apples.

"Hand me one of those," I said to Timmy.

"Gladly," he said, knowing exactly what I was about to do.

"Hey, Evan," I shouted. "Kiss this!"

And I reared back, wound up, and threw that caramel apple right into his . . . into his . . .

Well, you know where.

"ARRRGGH!" Evan screamed. He doubled over, fell off the chair, and landed in a heap on the ground, in the kind of pain only a caramel apple in the you-know-where can provide.

Everyone started laughing hysterically, because it was the kind of comedy only a caramel apple in the you-know-where can provide.

I looked at Zoe. I couldn't hear what she was saying, but I could read her lips. I think it was the first time I ever enjoyed reading.

"Nice shot," she said.

As all the kids gathered around to high-five me, I took a sip of my cream soda. Then it hit me. I was holding the can in my right hand. Which could mean only one thing.

I'd thrown the caramel apple with my left hand.

And it was a perfect strike.

My triumph didn't last very long, unfortunately.

The parents heard all the commotion and ran into the room. They were immediately followed by Mr. Twipple, who saw Evan doubled over in pain, while I was surrounded by kids congratulating me.

It didn't take him long to figure out what happened. He looked at me and shook his head.

"What happened to you tonight during the performance can happen to anyone. That's show business. But to take it out on a fellow actor is inexcusable. And it makes me question whether or not you're cut out for our Drama program. Which is really quite a shame, because you showed such promise."

As the adults helped Evan limp slowly out of the room, he managed to muster up enough energy to mumble one thing, right to me.

"Good luck getting that A, Jackson."

Part Five
AFTER ALL THAT . . .

Did I mention I hate Report Card Day? Even when it's the last day of school?

***

STUDENT: JACKSON, CHARLES JOSEPH
COUNSELOR: FERRELL, PATRICIA

ENGLISH: A–
ART: A
SOCIAL STUDIES: A
MATH: A–
SPANISH: A–
SCIENCE: B
GYM: A
DRAMA: C+

***

Camp Rituhbukkee, here I come.

There were only twenty minutes of school left before summer vacation, but I had one last stop to make.

Mr. Twipple was sitting at his desk, reading a book about some guy named Stephen Sondheim. He looked up when I came in.

"Mr. Jackson. How nice to see you."

I sat down. "I don't understand my grade."

"What is it you don't understand?"

"How could I get a C plus? I did everything you asked! I tried out for the play, I got a lead part, and I was really good. I don't get it!" I saw a pencil on the floor and tried to kick it, but missed. "Because of you, I'm going to have to spend my entire summer at a stupid camp for reading and writing."

He nodded. "You were very good indeed. Like I said, you have a great deal of talent. But the grade speaks for itself."

"It's all Evan Franco's fault," I muttered. "He's the one that psyched me out about kissing Hannah. And his toast was just mean."

Mr. Twipple sighed. "You're a smart boy, Charlie Joe," he said. "You just made some poor decisions."

As much as I hated to admit it, he was right. "I shouldn't have thrown that apple," I said. "I'm really sorry I let you down."

"But," Mr. Twipple added, "I will say this much. I believe you've found something that you're very good at. You gave a particularly fine performance. And you seemed to truly enjoy it."

It was true. I did feel something different when I was up on that stage. Something I'd never felt before. Something that felt pretty great.

"I regret what I said about you not being cut out for our Drama program," Mr. Twipple continued, "and I apologize for that. The truth is, I will be very disappointed if you don't continue with Drama in the future."

"Oh, I will," I said, hoping against hope that there was still a chance he'd change my grade. "I definitely will."

"And because you worked very hard, and you're a rookie who didn't know any better," Mr. Twipple continued, "I will indeed change your grade."

YES! My heart soared.

"To a B minus."

You know how parents get you to do something by pretending they don't care if you do it?

I hate that.

***

After my parents saw my report card, they didn't say anything for about five minutes. It felt like five years.

The suspense was killing me. My future hung in the balance. Well, at least, my immediate six-week future.

Then, finally, my dad looked up.

"Congratulations, Charlie Joe," he said. "This is a remarkable report card." And he hugged me.

My mom started grinning from ear to ear. "It's incredible!" And she hugged me, too.

"Really?" I asked. "You guys aren't mad that I didn't get straight A's?"

My dad laughed. "Are you kidding? See what you can do when you apply yourself? See what you can accomplish?"

"This calls for a celebration!" my mom announced. "I'm going to make a cake!"

Wow. I made my parents really, really happy. That was

a pretty cool feeling. Still, there was some unfinished business to attend to. But nobody seemed to want to finish it.

Since no one else was going to bring it up, I did.

"So . . . what about camp? Do I still have to go? I know we made a deal, but do I?"

My parents looked at each other. Then my dad shook his head.

"Nope. You don't have to go. Not if you don't want to."

"We wouldn't do that to you," agreed my mom. "You've worked so hard, you deserve to relax. What you do this summer is totally up to you."

I couldn't believe it. That was it. They'd said it. The words I'd been dying to hear. The words I'd worked so hard to make happen. Harder than I'd ever worked in my life. Harder than I would ever work again, if I had something to say about it.

But here's the thing. Something was wrong. For some reason I wasn't jumping up and down, celebrating.

Maybe it was because I'd never really made my parents proud like that before, and it was a pretty amazing feeling. Maybe it was because right after I'd made my parents really, really happy, all of a sudden they kind of looked a little sad. Or maybe it was because some part thought it actually might be a good idea to get away from my town and my friends and all the craziness that had happened over the last couple of months.

Whatever the reason, I suddenly heard someone say, "Well, maybe I should go anyway. Maybe it won't be so bad."

It took about a minute before I realized the person who had said that was me. Charlie Joe Jackson. The guy who'd posed for a painting in short shorts, broken a window, and froze like a deer in headlights in front of the whole school, just so he could avoid going to a summer camp for reading and writing. That Charlie Joe Jackson.

"Really?" asked my mom.

"Are you sure?" asked my dad.

I looked at them. I was pretty sure I would regret it for the rest of my life, but I nodded. "Yeah, I'm sure. If you guys think I should go, I'll go."

My mom gave me another hug, and I was pretty sure it was the biggest one she'd ever given me.

"I'm so proud of you," she said.

"Me, too," said my dad, who started hugging me, too.

As we all enjoyed the moment, it slowly started to dawn on me what I'd just gotten myself into.

It's weird how you can feel so good and so bad at the same time.

The day before I left for camp, I decided to torture myself by going to the second and last meeting of the Summer Planning Committee. I didn't have anything better to do; and besides, there was going to be Chinese food, which I've never been able to turn down for any reason.

This time the meeting was at Hannah's house. The whole gang was there: Timmy, Pete, Jake, Katie, Eliza, the Elizettes, and Nareem, who was going to the same camp I was—and completely looking forward to it.

Even Teddy Spivero, Hannah's horrifying twin brother, was there. He'd spent the year at a private school, where he got to irritate a whole new set of kids.

Zoe was there, too, of course.

She and I had decided that since I was going away to camp, it didn't make any sense to officially go out or anything. But that didn't mean we couldn't hang out with each other.

At this meeting, the committee actually got a lot of work done. Eliza was elected to organize a volleyball tournament. Katie started a sign-up sheet for volunteering at the homeless shelter once a week. Jake decided that they would all go to Six Flags on Fourth of July weekend.

And I decided that wanting to make your parents happy is a very, very dangerous thing.

***

During the meeting, Katie came and sat down next to me.

"You're being quiet."

I answered by being quiet.

"Any last words?"

I shook my head.

"I'm really impressed that you decided to go to camp after all, Charlie Joe", Katie said. "Could it be that you're actually, maybe, slightly growing up just a tiny bit?"

"Absolutely not," I answered.

She rolled her eyes, the way only she can roll them. "Fine. Anyway, it's not like you had it that bad this year anyway. I don't feel sorry for you, if that's what you're after."

I looked at her. "What do you mean?"

"Well, you posed for a painting and met a great girl who really likes you. Then you threw a baseball through Mrs. Sleep's window and didn't even get in trouble. And if all that's not enough, you got to be the star of the school play and kiss the girl you've been obsessed with for five years. On the lips!"

I guess if you put it that way, she had a point.

"Not to mention the fact that the whole time, the girl you were obsessed with was jealous of the girl you met in painting class," Katie added. "You basically had two awesome chicks fighting over you. So yeah, I'm gonna skip the whole feeling-sorry-for-you thing, if you don't mind."

And with that, she got up and walked away. Then she immediately turned around, ran back to me, and gave me a hug.

"So which is it?" she whispered. "Do you really like Zoe now? Or are you still obsessed with Hannah? Or do you want to take the summer to think about it?"

I thought for a second. "All of the above," I answered.

***

While we waited for the Chinese food, Hannah's brother Teddy decided it would be a good time to torture me.

"Yo, Jackson, I heard about your little freak-out during the show."

I didn't want to get into a who-can-be-a-bigger-jerk contest with him, since I knew he'd win. So I just nodded and said, "Yeah, a little bit."

"Well, at least you got to kiss Hannah, which we all know is a one-time offer," he said, giving me one of his special noogies.

Hannah saw what was going on and walked over. "Teddy, do you ever stop?" she said, pushing him away.

"Have a GREAT summer," Teddy offered as a parting shot.

Hannah smiled and shrugged. "Sorry about that."

I looked at her. I'd had something I'd wanted to say to her for a while, but I'd never really had the chance. Or maybe it was more like I'd never really had the nerve.

"So," I began, "the whole thing at the movie theater. That was—that was totally my fault."

"No, it wasn't," she said immediately. "You were right. I was jealous. Which didn't make any sense, because I didn't have any right to be. Which made me mad at myself for being jealous, and I took it out on you." She paused and smiled. "But being in the show with you was tons of fun."

"It was totally fun," I agreed.

She took a deep breath. "And Charlie Joe? I think I'm ready for you to like someone else now."

I took a deeper one. "I think I am, too."

She hugged me. "I really hope it works out with you and Zoe."

Then she walked away to find Jake.

***

When the food came, I sat next to Zoe.

"I'm really glad I met you this year," I said. I think Katie's whole "share your feelings" outlook on life was rubbing off of me.

Zoe looked at me, surprised. "I'm really glad I met you, too."

We ate in silence for a minute or two.

"Will you write to me?" she asked.

"Absolutely not. I'll be doing enough writing at this camp."

Zoe punched me. "Okay, fine. I won't write to you, either. But I'll send you a painting."

"Okay. And I'll send you a videotape of me reading a book. You can pass it around to the whole gang. It'll be the hit of the beach."

We both laughed, and without thinking, I kissed her.

On the lips. Just for a quick second.

Then she gave me one of those smiles.

"Let's eat," she said.

They had all my favorites: sesame chicken, beef with broccoli, and spare ribs. Life was good again.

At least for another twenty-four hours.

Charlie Joe's Tip #21

WHEN FINISHED WITH AN EXTRA CREDIT PROJECT, NEVER TALK ABOUT IT AGAIN.

Remember my very first tip? "Read a lot and work hard in school?" That's really the only way to avoid having to get extra credit. But since we all know that's never going to happen, good luck with your extra credit projects.

And then, after you're done, pretend it never happened.

Because the thing is, extra credit isn't something you really want to be bragging about. It's not even something to be proud of, really. It's something you do to survive. So get it done, and then move on. No one needs to know.

But sometimes, you get caught red-handed: like, someone saw you leaving school an hour after school ended, or something. When that happens, don't admit anything. Don't use the words *extra credit.* You'll just end up sounding like a brown-noser or an overachiever.

If you're really stuck, use my code word for extra credit.

Detention.

OUTRODUCTION

How I ended up trying out for the school play is actually a pretty funny story, right?

But I wasn't laughing on the drive up to Camp Rituh-bukkee.

It was the longest five hours of my life. All I kept thinking about was how I'd had one uncharacteristic moment of not putting myself first, and it was costing me my entire summer.

I'd never make that mistake again.

Finally we got there. It was way in the woods, with huge green pine trees and a bright blue lake.

Someone in a better mood than me probably would have called it beautiful.

People were walking around, talking. A couple of kids were swimming in the lake. Some were playing Frisbee.

From the outside, it looked like a normal camp, but I knew better.

"Look, honey!" my mom said.

She pointed to a big sign tacked to the door of the dining hall: TRYOUTS FOR THE CAMP MUSICAL TOMORROW NIGHT!

Okay, cool. That was something I could do. Maybe this wouldn't be so bad. Things were looking up. I could get used to people giving me standing ovations. I might even have a semi-decent time at this place.

Then I noticed the name of the show.

Read-A-Rama! A Musical in Three Chapters.

Holy moly. This was going to be the longest summer of my life.

As I started walking toward the registration tent, I heard someone call my name.

"Charlie Joe! Charlie Joe!"

Nareem was running towards me, huffing and puffing.

"Charlie Joe! You made it!"

"Yup," I said. "Can't wait to get started."

"Great!" Nareem said, completely missing my sarcasm. Then he looked over my shoulder and pointed. "Hey, guess who else decided to come to camp this year?"

I turned around, but didn't see anybody. I started

wondering who it was. Did Zoe decide to surprise me by coming to camp? No way! Or maybe it was Hannah? *Hannah? But I didn't like her any more! Or did I?* My mind started to race, considering the possibilities . . . Hannah? Zoe? Zoe? Hannah?

Then I saw her.

Katie Friedman.

She was walking toward me, dragging a duffel bag and smiling.

"Hi," she said.

"Hi!" I said back. "What are you doing here?"

"I decided I wanted to read some bookies," she said. "And maybe even I'll get you to like some bookies, too."

"I doubt that," I said, hugging her.

She went over to say hi to my parents. Watching her, I realized that spending the summer at camp with Hannah or Zoe would have been *way* too complicated.

But spending the summer with Katie was perfect.

"Wait, so I don't get it. Why are you here?" I asked her. "Is it just because you're smart and you want to get smarter? Is it because of Nareem? Or is it because you actually really did feel a little sorry for me and didn't want me to have a sad lonely summer?"

She hoisted her duffel bag up onto her shoulder and looked me straight in the eye.

"All of the above," Katie Friedman said.

Charlie Joe's Special Bonus Tip:

YOU CAN AVOID EXTRA CREDIT IF YOU REALLY WANT TO.

This book is about getting extra credit. But I wouldn't have written it if I didn't have to get extra credit in the first place. And that probably would have been a whole lot easier.

Here are some of the ways you can avoid having to get extra credit:

1. *If your teacher makes a joke, don't make a funnier joke right after.*
2. *Don't come in late to class and claim, "All of the clocks in this school are wrong."*
3. *Don't try and pay for lunch with Monopoly money.*
4. *In Gym, don't try to dunk a real basketball into a Nerf hoop.*
5. *Eat your lunch during Lunch, not Math.*
6. *Remember that Science is not recess.*
7. *"I want to be a professional finger-painter" is not a legitimate reason for getting into a paint fight in Art class.*
8. *Be the opposite of me.*

THE FINALE OF "PAPER TIGER: THE LIFE AND LEGEND OF ARTHUR SCOTT"

Music and Lyrics by Jeffrey Twipple

Arthur Scott and Fred Wimple enter a giant forest. Arthur looks at a map that's in his hand.

ARTHUR

Here we are. *(He looks around.)* See this, Fred? All these trees? Think of them as giant rolls of paper towels, giant napkins waiting to be folded. And all this is ours!

FRED

What do you mean?

ARTHUR

I just bought this land, Fred. I just bought it for twenty-two dollars from a couple of Native American fellows.

FRED

You are such a brilliant man, Arthur!

ARTHUR

Stop it.

FRED

No, seriously, you are.

ARTHUR

I couldn't have done it without you, my former enemy and now good friend.

FRED

Funny how life works.

ARTHUR

Indeed.

As they shake hands, there is a thundering sound. Suddenly a tree falls and just misses them.

ARTHUR

My goodness, what on earth was it.

FRED

I have no idea!

Suddenly William "Big Bill" Brawny, their arch

rival, emerges from behind the tree with a big ax.

BILL

Not so fast, gentleman.

FRED

It's William "Big Bill" Brawny! And he's looking bigger and brawnier than ever!

ARTHUR

(To Fred) Let me handle this.

BILL

I'm not giving up without a fight.

ARTHUR

Bill, we bought this land fair and square. These are our trees, which will soon become our paper. If you want to take it, you'll have to pry it out of my cold dead hands.

BILL

Are you sure about that?

Bill puts down his ax and takes out a gun. Arthur bravely stands his ground.

ARTHUR

I've never been more sure of anything in my entire life.

BILL

Fine. It's your funeral. And soon, it will be my forest.

As Bill is about to pull the trigger, Arthur's wife Mary runs on stage with their ten-year-old son, Little Jack.

MARY

Wait! No! Stop!

Mary runs in front of Arthur, preventing Bill from shooting.

MARY

Mr. Brawny, please don't kill my husband!

BILL

If you'll kindly get of my way, Mrs.

Scott. It's just business, nothing personal.

MARY

But you don't understand! Arthur is everything to me! And our little boy! You can't let him grow up without a father!

BILL

Then get married again. Come on, move! I don't have all day.

What Bill doesn't realize is that while he's been arguing with Mary, Little Jack has run up behind him. Suddenly Jack jumps on Bill and covers his eyes.

BILL

Argh!! What's that?!? What's going on? Who's there?

LITTLE JACK

It's me, Little Jack Scott! And I have some news for you: NOBODY messes with my dad.

They continue to struggle, with Little Jack grabbing Bill's arm. As Arthur runs up to help his son, the gun suddenly goes off! For a few horrible seconds, we don't know who's been shot. Then, Bill screams.

BILL

OW!!! My foot! My foot! I've been shot! My foot!

Fred goes over to look at Bill's wound.

FRED

Indeed you have. You have shot yourself in the foot. *(Fred thinks to himself for a minute.)* Hey, that's catchy. I should turn that into a common expression someday . . .

Little Jack Jumps off Bill's back and runs into his father's arms.

LITTLE JACK

Dad!

ARTHUR

Little Jack!

MARY

Arthur! Little Jack!

The three of them hug, then go over to Bill and Fred. Arthur kneels down to talk to Bill.

ARTHUR

Do you promise to respect me on my land? Do you promise to respect the earth, and the trees, and the extra-absorbent materials they hold within?

BILL

I do. I'm sorry, I don't know what I was thinking. I should have respected you and your remarkable all-American success story of determination, innovation, and hard work.

ARTHUR

Good. Then I'll help you.

Arthur and Fred look at Bill's foot, which now has blood coming out of it.

FRED

We've got to find something to clean up this mess.

Arthur winks at Little Jack.

ARTHUR

I know just the thing.

Arthur gives Fred a roll of paper towels, and Fred and Little Jack help Bill off stage. Left alone in the forest, Mary and Arthur look into each other's eyes. The music starts as they sing.

ARTHUR

LESSONS WORTH ABSORBING
ARE THE MOST IMPORTANT LESSONS OF ALL.
LOVE AND FAMILY
AND LEARNING HOW TO STAND TALL.

MARY

LESSONS WORTH ABSORBING
ARE A GIFT FROM UP ABOVE.
AND THE MOST ABSORBING LESSON OF ALL
IS LEARNING HOW TO LOVE.

ARTHUR

Everything I've done in this world . . . everything I've accomplished . . . I've done for you and Little Jack.

MARY

You have given so much to us. And now, you have given paper towels to the world. I am so proud of you.

ARTHUR

I love you.

MARY

I love you, too.

They kiss. Suddenly, the entire cast comes out from behind the trees. Everyone sings . . . even Big Bill.

ALL

LESSONS WORTH ABSORBING
ARE WHAT MAKES THE WORLD GO ROUND.
EVERY THING WE DO AND TOUCH
EVERY SIGHT AND EVERY SOUND.
LESSONS WORTH ABSORBING
TAUGHT TO EVERY BOY AND GIRL

WILL BE THE ONLY WAY
WE CAN CLEAN UP THIS WORLD.

Little Jack walks to the front of the stage, where his father had dropped his map earlier. He turns it around and on the other side is a map of the entire world. As he dances, he takes a paper towel out of his pocket and wipes the map clean. The cast all hold hands and come to the edge of the stage to surround Arthur, Mary, and Little Jack.

ALL

LESSONS WORTH ABSORBING
TAUGHT TO EVERY BOY AND GIRL
WILL BE THE ONLY WAY
WE CAN CLEAN UP THIS WORLD.

The lights slowly fade to black.

END OF SHOW

ACKNOWLEDGMENTS

Extra credit goes to the following:

Michele Rubin and Nan Mercado, the brain trust.

Lizzy Mason, Kathryn Hurley, Andrew Arnold, Jill Freshney, Patricia Egan, and everyone at Roaring Brook/ Macmillan for their wonderfulness.

Meghan Ownbey for caring so much.

Cameron Skene for teaching me how to speak internet.

Aaliytha Davis for the freebies.

Chris, Katie, Andy, Mary Lou, Kristen, Sally and Tracy, my invaluable critique group partners.

The Elevensies—brave and hearty souls all—and all my new, fantastic, passionate, never-met-'em online friends.

Tish Gayle, Joshua Newhouse, and Joan Kindig, champions of children's literacy.

Micheal Arroyo, one of Charlie Joe's first real-world pals.

All the usual suspects I named last time.

And of course, the fam.